What the c

On *Sins of the Father*:

"An emotionally charged, sexual rush... Ms. Black's writing is superb in SINS OF THE FATHER. Her in-depth characters, her hot love scenes and the storyline make [it] hard to put down... definitely not one to be missed." - *Michelle Gann, The Word on Romance*

"Jaid Black returns to erotic romance with this doozy of a story. Hot, sexy and spell-bindingly explicit, SINS OF THE FATHER explodes across the screen...a story sure to please fans." – *Ann Leveille for Sensual Romance (referencing original e-book edition)*

On *Surrender*:

"Lora Leigh packs a lot into this short tale. This is a highly sexual and emotionally charged novella." - *Sara Sawyer, The Romance Studio*

"This is the best of erotic writing...[SURRENDER] expands boundaries beyond your own experiences and preferences to understanding alternative fantasies." - *Karen Williston for Sensual Romance*

Discover for yourself why readers can't get enough of the multiple award-winning publisher Ellora's Cave. Whether you prefer e-books or paperbacks, be sure to visit EC on the web at www.ellorascave.com for an erotic reading experience that will leave you breathless.

www.ellorascave.com

Ellora's Cave Publishing, Inc.
PO Box 787
Hudson, OH 44236-0787

ISBN # 1-84360-619-4

"Sins Of The Father" edited by Cris Brashear.
"Surrender" edited by Kari Berton.
Cover art by Darrell King.

Warning: The following material contains strong sexual content meant for mature readers. *Ties That Bind* has been rated NC-17, erotic, by a minimum of six independent reviewers. We strongly suggest storing this book in a place where young readers not meant to view it are unlikely to happen upon it. That said, enjoy…

TIES THAT BIND

Sins Of The Father
by Jaid Black
~7~

Surrender
by Lora Leigh
~93~

SINS OF THE FATHER

Written by

Jaid Black

To my grandmother, Janet, who, apparently unappeased by the fact I named two heroines and my own child after her, insisted I also dedicate a story to her. Done! (Just don't read past the dedication, Gramma — take my word for it that I write sweet, G-rated romances. This is your baby talking and I can be trusted. Really.)

You are the ultimate battleaxe, the Julia Child of Jell-O salad, an Olympic champion nag, the only short chick in the world who can get away with jabbing me in the knees with her cane without dire retaliation...and I love you to bits :)

Chapter 1

"Excu-use me?" Candy Morgan stuttered out. Her amber eyes widened as she regarded the man sitting across from her at the expensive mahogany oak desk. She couldn't have heard him correctly. There was no way in the hell that—

"You heard me," he murmured. His intense blue gaze bore into hers, his expression brooding. "I won't repeat myself."

Candy stared at him open mouthed, too stunned to speak. She couldn't believe what she was hearing, couldn't believe that this man, James Douglas Mahoney III, was suggesting—no *demanding*—the things that he was. Under any other circumstances she would have said yes. Under these circumstances her pride would only allow her to say…

"No." She shook her head, swallowing roughly as she looked at him. "I won't be used like that, JD. I can't believe you'd suggest such a thing," she whispered.

His eyebrows rose, but otherwise he remained calmly stoic. His arrogant gaze wandered up and down the length of her body, all but disrobing her from the demure white silk blouse and matching white skirt she wore. So much for the casual lunch they were supposed to be having, she thought. There was nothing casual about the way he was attempting to dominate the situation.

Her teeth gritted when she considered just how much the bastard was probably enjoying her discomfort. But then, could she blame him? If the circumstances were reversed, she didn't know how she'd be treating him.

JD Mahoney, she sighed. The man who had been the focal point of more adolescent wet dreams than she could count had finally noticed her as a woman. At the age of thirty, she had waited a long, long time for this moment to be realized. But now that it was here, she morosely considered, she had to turn him down. The irony was not lost on her.

At forty, he was still as handsome, if not more handsome, than he'd been the first time she'd laid eyes on him when she'd been but thirteen. She had fallen instantly in love with the then twenty-three-year-old, but even so she'd been socially adept enough to realize that it was and would always be a one-sided attraction.

Men who looked like JD Mahoney didn't settle for women who looked like Candy Morgan.

Not even when that woman was the daughter of the wealthiest man in Atlanta, Georgia.

Candy supposed she'd aged well enough. She had an exotic, pretty enough face with amber eyes that were turned up a bit at the corners, full lips, a cheerful smile, long blonde curls, and a slight southern drawl. But she'd never been skinny, not even at her best, and she'd certainly never been tall.

If there was one thing Candy had learned growing up amongst la crème de la crème of society, it was that handsome, powerful men wanted gorgeous, tall, beanpole, trophy wives. They wanted the women who ate lettuce without dressing and drank mineral water and called that a meal—not women who passionately dined on steaks and baked potatoes (loaded with butter and sour cream, of course), drank sugared sodas, and enjoyed it all without a qualm. They wanted the women with limbs long enough to wrap around a tree trunk—not a woman whose legs were shorter than felled stumps.

She sighed. Delicately feminine she'd never be.

"You do what you need to do," Candy quietly said as she rose from the chair. She nervously ran her sweaty palms down the front of her designer skirt, her gaze purposely avoiding his. She would not be a whore for any man—not even for the only man she'd ever really wanted. "And I'll do what I need to do," she said with more staunch than she felt. "I believe I should leave now."

Candy walked towards the office door, then stopped mid-stride. She turned her head, gazing at him from over her shoulder. "Regardless to what you decide to do," she said softly, "I am and have always been against what my father did to you." His stark eyes seemed to widen a bit, but she couldn't be sure. "And I'm not just saying that."

Indeed, she had been JD's most vocal champion. When her father had turned against his young protégé, dropping him like soiled goods to earn a quick buck, she had been mortified. It had taken quite a long time before she was able to forgive him and continue on as a father and daughter should. Even then, it had been a few more years before the strain between them had eased.

"Goodbye, JD," she whispered, striding towards the door. She sighed, wishing things had never come to this, wishing too that she could have lived out her fantasies of being in his bed without doing it by serving as the familial sacrifice. But in JD Mahoney's eyes, she knew, one of the Morgans had to pay for the father's sins. And since the father was dead and she now owned Morgan Chemicals outright, there was only one woman who could pay for them.

She made it to the heavy double doors of the posh office and was preparing to open them when a rough palm slapped against the wood beam above her head and didn't budge. She nervously gulped, able to feel the heat radiating off of the six-foot one-inch body that was pressed against hers from behind. He was aroused, she could tell. Whether by her as a woman or by the power he held over her — or both — she couldn't say.

"Think about what you're doing, Candy," he murmured. "Your mother and brother are relying on you to make the best decision for everyone involved."

She was torn between arousal and anger. Arousal both because his body was pressed against hers...and because it was the first time she'd ever heard him use the more familiar "Candy" as opposed to "Candace" when speaking to her. Anger because he had just presumed that her mother and brother were as greedy as her father had been. Anger won out.

"My mother," she ground out, "would never condone allowing myself to be used like a common prostitute." Her nostrils flared. "And neither would my brother for that matter."

"I see," JD growled from next to her ear. She could feel those intense, intelligent eyes of his boring into the back of her skull. Analyzing. Assessing. Calculating. That's what he did best. That's why, unlike the hundreds of other former employees her father had screwed over, James Douglas Mahoney III had managed to fight his way back to the top and now held the upper hand over her today.

"But what do *you* think is best, my dear Candy?" His free hand came to rest on her shoulder, rubbing it, caressing it. "What executive decision do you think is best for *you* to make today? Your family can lose so much. Or," he finished, "I can let bygones be bygones and your family, corrupt though it might be, will be permitted to carry on as they always have."

Candy's body stilled. "You want me to be your whore," she said quietly. "Regardless to what you might think of my family, I was raised better than that."

"You were daddy's little girl," he murmured against her ear. He pressed closer, his thick erection poking against her back. She blew out a breath. "I have no doubt that Lawrence raised you to be everything he was not."

Which made JD's revenge against the Morgan family all the sweeter to him, she thought glumly. She was sweet and innocent in his eyes — a true lady of elite breeding.

And a true sacrificial lamb in every sense of the word.

Her spine stiffened. Suddenly it all made sense. Suddenly she understood why it was that this man who had everything, this man who could possess any woman of his choosing, wanted her to play mistress to him...

Because she was nothing like her father. And because he was hoping that Lawrence Morgan, his betrayer, would somehow know from the grave that JD Mahoney had managed to turn his beloved Candace into the same person Lawrence had been while alive — a proverbial whore who would do anything for a dollar.

"What do you want me to do?" she ground out. "Have sex with you? How many times? When would it end?" She spun around on her heel, her eyes blazing into his. At over six feet, he stood almost a full foot taller than her own five-two so she had to push him back a bit before she could meet his gaze, but she was too angry to be intimidated by that fact. "How much of you would I be forced to stomach?" she spat out.

JD smiled, an arrogant gesture designed to further infuriate her. It worked.

"Well?" she shrieked. "Get on with your demands! I can't put my family out on the street when I have the power to stop it and you damn well know it. So tell me what the hell it is you want from me," she seethed, "and be done with it."

He chuckled, his intense blue eyes roaming over every square inch of her body. His gaze stopped at her breasts before continuing onward to her face. "I want more than sex from you, Candy," he said softly. Too softly. "I want everything."

She swallowed against the lump in her throat. "What exactly does that mean?" she asked a bit weakly. "I'm not in the mood to solve riddles."

His dark eyebrows rose, but he said nothing. He stuffed his hands in the pockets of the expensive Italian suit he wore and intently regarded her face. "Everything," he murmured, "means just that." His jaw clenched. "Sex isn't good enough, my dear. Not good enough by a long shot."

She blushed, feeling like a fool that she'd thought for even a moment that JD Mahoney wanted her in his bed. What a ridiculous notion, she conceded. She bit her lip. He could have any woman he wanted. He hardly needed to get his rocks off with ordinary her.

"Oh don't think you're off the hook," he growled, misinterpreting the look she'd given him as relief. "I'll be fucking you whenever and however I want. But sex is only a small part of the overall penance, *darling*."

She hesitated, worry engulfing her features once again. "What precisely do you mean?" she muttered. "You've lost me."

"I'm going to own you," he said simply, coming straight to the point. His gaze drilled into hers, his expression once again brooding. "Marry you, breed you, have total control over your body—"

Her amber eyes widened. That was the last thing she had been expecting to hear. *Marry her?* He didn't need to marry her to take over Morgan Chemicals! At this juncture, all it would take was one word to the bank and board of directors and it was all his.

"—and Lawrence will know from the grave that not only have I succeeded in infiltrating his precious company, but I have also succeeded in infiltrating his goddamn bloodline."

Candy stared at him blankly, too stunned to react. JD's grand plan went beyond anything she could have ever fathomed. It went beyond it, circumnavigated it, and then crash-landed into the realm of surreality. "Are you insane?" she whispered. "You can't possibly want to marry me. Why would you sentence us both to a lifetime of—"

"Question and answer period is over," he arrogantly announced. One dark eyebrow shot up. "You have two choices, my dear. Come under my ownership and I allow your family to live in peace. Or reject the chance I am offering you to save their livelihoods and lose everything in the process. The choice is yours." His gaze flicked down to her breasts, then back up to her face. "Make it and make it quickly."

She blinked, barely able to form a coherent thought let alone make a life-altering decision. "Why do you call it ownership? Marriage isn't exactly ownership—"

"Mine will be."

Mine. Not *ours.* The possessive word hadn't been lost on her.

JD's calculating eyes flicked down once more, grazing over her body. "You will fuck me as often as I want and however I want it. You will cater to my every whim and fulfill my every perverted fantasy." Her body responded to his words, becoming aroused against her volition. "You will bear as many of my children as I say. You will behave as I say. You will never touch nor look at another man in a sexual way..." His gaze shot up to penetrate hers. "I will own you," he murmured. "Completely."

She swallowed roughly, her eyes wide.

"Give me your decision, Miss Morgan." His jaw was firm, his eyes harsh. "The clock, and my patience, is ticking."

* * * * *

Dazed was the only word that came to mind to describe how she was currently feeling. An hour after she accepted the ultimatum she'd been given, her lawyer had arrived in JD's office at Candy's behest. Robert, her family's attorney, had flown into a rage when reading the terms of the prenuptial agreement, arguing that it would never hold up in court. JD's lawyer had argued to the contrary, pointing out that a prenuptial agreement could contain *any* clause so long as both parties agreed to it in writing.

In the end, JD had firmly insisted that not a word of the document would be altered or the deal was off. Robert took her aside and privately informed her that his hands were tied and the decision was hers. Candy, not knowing what else to do, had signed the wretched thing, probably against her better judgment.

Not even five minutes after she'd caved in, JD had steered her into an adjoining room where a judge was waiting to make it all official. A bit *too* planned out to her way of thinking. So methodical, in fact, that she found herself wondering just how long JD Mahoney had plotted against her. She had always known him to be calculating, but this required a patience that bordered on inhuman.

Everything was happening so fast—too fast. Her opponent wasn't giving her time to think, which, she begrudgingly admitted, was probably a smart tactical move on his part.

"Do you, Candace Marie Morgan, take this man..."

Good lord, she thought, her lips working up and down in an effort to answer the question, this was insane—simply insane. As a little girl, she had often daydreamed about standing next to JD Mahoney and doing this very thing. But under the current circumstances?

This wedding ceremony felt more like a nightmare than the realization of an adolescent fantasy.

And why was this marriage taking place to begin with? she asked herself for about the fiftieth time in the last hour. No matter what angle she looked at the situation from, it made no sense. She could understand JD wanting revenge. She could not understand him wanting to marry her to obtain it.

Ownership, she recalled him saying. He wanted to own her. She supposed in some bizarre way this gave him the revenge he sought, but it still didn't explain why he'd decided matrimony was requisite to seeing it through.

"I do," JD muttered from beside her, gaining him her full, wide-eyed attention. The hand at the base of her back gently nudged her. "Say 'I do'."

She swallowed, her heart thumping like a rock in her chest. "I do," Candy breathed out. She blinked, briefly glancing at the judge before looking back to JD. "I do," she repeated.

The look of arrogance on her husband-to-be's face made her teeth gnash together. She would get out of this, she told herself, her nostrils flaring as she turned her attention on the judge. Somehow, some way, some day, she would find a way out of this farce — without her family getting tossed onto the streets of Atlanta in the process. She clung to that goal like a mental talisman, using it like a crutch to help her through the remainder of the ceremony.

Candy closed her eyes and took a steadying breath as the judge said the words that legally bound them together. She had never felt closer to fainting in her entire life. Fainting, or she thought grimly as her eyes opened and clashed with a certain arrogant male's, murdering. Fainting and murdering were two very disparate actions, yet both of them seemed rather apropos to the situation.

One of JD's eyebrows inched up as he took in her expression. His smile came slowly, but fully. "There now," he said in a patronizing tone of voice, "that wasn't so bad, was it?"

The seething look she threw him didn't dent his satisfaction in the slightest, though his jaw did tighten somewhat. "Let's go," he instructed, his hand at the base of her back as he guided her from the room. "It's time for me to take my *wife* on a little honeymoon."

Candy's expression went from angry to worried in a heartbeat. She hoped he was being sarcastic and not literal. The word honeymoon implied leaving Atlanta — something she couldn't do if she hoped to work behind the scenes to get her company back. "What do you mean?" she asked hesitantly, her body stilling.

"A honeymoon," he said dryly. "That thing people go on after they get married." He patted her butt, making her yelp. "Let's go."

Chapter 2

Candy hesitantly accepted JD's hand, her mouth dry as cotton when he laced his larger fingers through hers and guided her towards his private, corporate airplane. She hadn't been expecting that they'd have a real honeymoon—not by a long shot. So she'd been surprised, and more than a little worried, when her husband of an hour had informed her that they were heading for his private tropical island off the coast of Costa Rica and that they would remain there for two months.

The thought was arousing.

The thought was distressing.

There would be no one around to hear her screams if he meant to do her any harm.

Logically speaking, he didn't seem the type who got off on inflicting pain on others, but then again, who was she to say? She barely knew him. Besides, she thought morosely, she was aware of the fact that he believed her to have been in cahoots with her father. She doubted that her softly whispered words to the contrary in his office, words that had come five years too late, had made much of a difference. She sighed, wondering again what he meant to do with her.

And, damn it anyway, there was no way to fight him once they left Atlanta. She needed to be there to keep tabs on the take-over...and find ways to reverse it. Her lawyer had advised her that the situation looked hopeless, but hopeless had never stopped Candy before. She needed to find a way to get back to Atlanta — and she had to do it with the arrogant jerk's permission.

JD had actually made her compliance toward him a legal part of their marriage. She had been all but forced to sign the prenuptial agreement, swearing by penalty of her family being expelled from their familial estate that she would obey him without question in all things. Legally, she recalled through gritted teeth, she wasn't even allowed to raise her voice to him without her family being punished. Not if she wished to keep from violating the damn contract he'd insisted she sign.

Her nostrils flared. She had a feeling her family would be tossed into the streets outside of a week. Contrary to JD's beliefs, she had never been the sweet, biddable type. Sweet, biddable women couldn't effectively run billion dollar companies. And she *had* effectively run it before the takeover. Problem being her father had made a lot of foolish business decisions before his death that had depleted a great deal of capital.

Then again, her "husband" probably knew that. She silently wondered if that was part of the lure of marrying her — getting a chance to forcibly bring a strong, independent woman to heel after slowly bleeding her cash assets dry so she could no longer fight him.

Thirty minutes later, the plane had taken off, the cocktails had been served, and Candy sat in her seat across from her new husband sipping on a margarita. She stared out of the window, pretending to watch the clouds pass by, too overwhelmed to make eye contact with the man who for all intent and purposes held all power over her.

Still, her intelligence hadn't deserted her. Even if she wasn't looking at him, she knew that he was watching her — staring at her. The knowledge of it put her senses on alert, fraying her already wrought nerves. For years she had wanted to be the object of this man's attention. Now she was and she didn't know how to feel. Her mind abhorred his focus on her, but her damn belly was clenching in a weird way. Apparently her mind hadn't yet informed her butterfly-filled stomach that the attention she was currently the brunt of was not a positive thing.

"You have gorgeous breasts," JD murmured, gaining him her full wide-eyed attention. She hadn't expected him to be so forthwith — why, she hadn't a clue. Forthwith was in his nature. "I can see how stiff your nipples are from under your blouse." He watched as she nervously cleared her throat and glanced away. "Are you cold, aroused, or both?"

Aroused, she thought, squirming a bit in her seat. "Cold," she whispered.

Candy briefly closed her eyes, steeling herself. Perverse or not, stupid or not, her body had always innately responded to the dark, forbidding man sitting across from her. It was as if her body had been created by the gods for the sole purpose of finding pleasure with James Douglas Mahoney III. No other man had gotten her aroused from mere words and simple glances. No other man but JD.

She hated to admit it, but he looked more dangerously handsome than ever today. Still wearing the same Italian black suit he'd married her in, his dark brown hair was as attractively disheveled as the tie that he'd loosened and which now laid haphazardously slung around his neck. His athletic musculature was evident even with clothing covering his body. His eyes were deep blue and intense, the laugh lines at the corners in stark contrast to the brooding expression on his face.

"Then I'll have to change that," he said softly, setting down his brandy. "I want my wife aroused for me and my cock at all times."

Candy blew out a breath, squelching the reaction to gawk at him. As taken aback as she was, arousal still overwhelmed her. This was just too much. It didn't matter to her libido that all JD wanted from her was revenge. This was still the same man she'd secretly yearned for over half of her life.

She was already turned on, she conceded. If he touched her she would probably explode on contact. She firmly reminded herself that she had no business being aroused, that this man whom she had desired for so many years was, after all, the same man who had taken her life as she knew it away from her. She'd have to keep remembering that fact.

"Take off your clothes."

Her head shot up to meet his gaze. Her eyes rounded. "Wh-What?" she breathed out. Her heart felt as though it might thump out of her chest. He was wasting no time in upping the ante.

JD's intense blue eyes grew impossibly more so. "Take off your clothes," he repeated.

"B-But the crew —"

"Your clothes," he said softly, his look reminding her of their legal marriage agreement. "Take them off."

Candy stilled. She had never permitted a man to see what she looked like naked in the full light of day. Contemplating doing so was the most frightening thing she could imagine. And yet, perversely, it was also the most arousing.

She really wished her libido would get with the program. JD wanted revenge — not her.

"I'm waiting," he murmured. "I want to see those stiff nipples of yours with no clothing on to impede my view."

She quickly chugged the remainder of the margarita, then set the glass down. She hesitated for a moment, but inevitably, stood up and prepared to undress herself. It wasn't as if she had much choice in the matter, Candy reminded herself. She would have to comply for as long as she could, or at least until she figured a way out of this mess. If such a way even existed. She might become an alcoholic first, she grimly decided.

"Would you turn around?" she asked quietly, her head bowed in embarrassment. "Please?"

"No." JD picked up his brandy and settled comfortably into his seat.

Candy glanced up, for some reason surprised by the obvious arousal in his voice. She quickly averted her gaze, immediately noting the prominent bulge in his trousers. She blew out a breath.

"I want to look at my wife, not at the back of the goddamn plane," he said thickly.

Her teeth sank into her lower lip. Painful recollections of her father telling her that she needed to lose weight, that she was too fat and unappealing, flooded her memories. *Go to the gym and work out*, Lawrence had repeatedly told her. *You'll never snag a husband looking like a heifer out to pasture.*

"I'm not much to look at," Candy whispered. "Please...I'm not trying to go back on our deal, but I — "

"I think you have everything to look at," he interrupted, surprising her. "Now show it to me. I want to see the nipples I now own...and the rest of the body that belongs to me."

She took a calming breath, his words more arousing than ten knowing hands intimately massaging her all at

23

once. She didn't want to be attracted to him, given the circumstances of their marriage, but there it was. It was hard not to be attracted to a handsome man who was, whether he realized it or not, making her feel like maybe, just maybe, she wasn't as completely unappealing as she'd always thought.

Candy slowly began peeling off her clothing. She carefully avoided making eye contact, but could feel his intense gaze all over her when she removed first her white silk blouse and then her lacy white bra.

His hands immediately seized her breasts, making her gasp in shock. His thumbs massaged her distended nipples. "Beautiful," he murmured, his voice thick. "Your nipples are large and long. Perfect for sucking on."

She squeezed her thighs together and blew out a breath. His mouth was so close to her nipples she could feel his breath warming them. "Th-Thank you."

His tongue lashed out, surprising her, making her gasp again. He took turns with both breasts, slowly licking around the circumference of each nipple, then suctioning the tip into his mouth.

Her heart rate went over the top, her legs beginning to feel like overcooked spaghetti noodles. He curled his tongue around her left nipple and drew it into the heat of his mouth. She moaned softly when his lips latched onto it, her hands instinctively threading through his dark hair as he began to suckle it.

JD spent the next ten minutes showering her breasts with attention. He sucked on one nipple for a couple of minutes, then switched to the other one and did the same. He repeated the process over and over again, not stopping until she was breathless and clinging to him.

His dark head came up from her chest, his eyelids heavy. "Now the rest," he murmured. "Show me the exquisite cunt I now own."

Her breathing labored, her nipples achingly swollen, Candy complied. She stepped back a bit as her hands shakily reached behind her for the zipper to her white, thigh-high skirt. She glanced down at her breasts as she unzipped herself, noting how ruby-red and distended her nipples were. She could still see the faint outline of teeth marks, a sight that made her wetter still.

"Now remove your panties," JD said hoarsely as her skirt fell to the ground and pooled around her feet. "I want you wearing nothing but those high heels."

The white silk panties came off next, quickly joining the garments already laying on the ground. She heard JD suck in his breath and wasn't sure what to make of the sound. She bit into her lower lip, once again feeling ashamed and unsure of her body. Was he aroused or disgusted? She couldn't tell. She shouldn't care.

He stilled. "You shaved your pussy bald," he said thickly. "Have you always shaved it bald?"

She nodded, still too embarrassed to look him in the eye.

"Why?" he murmured. "Do you like how sensitive it is when you masturbate yourself?"

Her face grew hot, giving him her answer. She looked away.

"Show me," he said, his tone commanding. "Sit down, spread your legs, and show me how you like to touch yourself."

"JD—"

"Show me," he cut her off, interrupting her protest. "Your body belongs to me now, Candy. From here on out, you use it to pleasure your husband, not yourself."

. She blew out a breath. The man had a way with words. Candy knew this was destined to be the shortest masturbation session of her life for she was already this close to coming. "Okay," she whispered.

Sitting down in her seat across from him, Candy splayed her legs wide, bringing them down to rest on the arms of the seat. She could feel his commanding eyes staring boldly at her exposed flesh, his gaze practically branding it.

"Touch yourself," he said thickly.

He unzipped his trousers and released his erection from its previous confinement. She swallowed as she briefly stared at it. His cock was long and thick, a vein running prominently down the middle from the root to the head.

"Play with your cunt for me."

Her fingers slid down and found her clit. She bit her lip as she watched him stare at her through hooded eyes. She closed her eyes and began to manipulate her clit, rubbing it in a circular fashion as her breathing grew more and more labored.

"That's right, sweetheart," he said in low tones. "Keep stroking your pussy for me. From now on you always have to ask my permission before you touch yourself. Do you understand me, Candy?"

From somewhere in the back of her fevered mind she found the wherewithal to answer yes.

"It's my cunt now," he possessively reminded her. "And it's never to be touched without the permission of its owner."

Candy gasped as desire shot through her, knotting in her belly. She continued to rub her fingers all over her drenched clit, the swollen piece of flesh throbbing with blood, aching for release.

"Beautiful," JD murmured, his voice aroused. "Exquisite."

She came on a loud groan, blood rushing up to heat her face. Her nipples shot out, distended and swollen. Her breath came out in pants.

A knock on the cabin door made Candy yelp, bringing her back to reality quicker than a bucket of ice water to the face.

One of JD's eyebrows rose. "Don't get dressed," he ordered her when she reached for her blouse. "There's a blanket in the cabinet to your right. Use it while I see what my assistant wants."

The thought horrified her. "But I don't want him to see—"

"He won't see anything," he interrupted her. His erection was very obvious, very swollen against his trousers. "Just get the blanket."

Her heart racing, she moved quicker than what she thought she was capable of. Blanketed from neck to toes within seconds, she thought she saw a bemused expression cross his face before his features went blank and he called out to his assistant that it was okay to come in.

Candy blew out a breath as Tom entered the cabin and the two men began discussing business matters she cared nothing about. His assistant was trying not to look at her, she could tell, but his gaze kept repeatedly flicking to where she sat. She blushed, remembering how loudly she'd climaxed only seconds before Tom had knocked on the door. She wondered if he'd heard her and supposed that he probably had.

"That will be all for now," she heard JD mutter to his assistant. She bit her lip, watching as her husband was handed a refill of brandy. "Don't come in here again before the plane lands."

"Of course, Mr. Mahoney."

Tom walked away, his face stoic but the bulge in his pants telling another story. Good lord, he *had* heard her, Candy thought, horrified. She wanted to die of embarrassment. It was unlikely the assistant was aroused simply because she was sitting here wearing a blanket— she'd seen nuns wearing less material! Besides, he couldn't have known she was naked beneath it unless he heard what she had been doing before he came in. The temperature in the plane was on the chilly side. Under ordinary circumstances most people would have just assumed she was cold.

JD narrowed his eyes at her. She blinked, having no clue as to why.

"Never look at another man's penis," he snapped.

Candy gritted her teeth. "Why did you let Tom come in here if I wasn't supposed to notice his reaction to the events he'd obviously overheard!" Her gaze found his. She couldn't stop her nostrils from flaring, her anger from showing a bit. "Why did you let him in here?"

He smiled slightly. "Truthfully?"

She frowned. "Well, yes."

"Truthfully, I didn't realize he'd heard anything until he was in here and I saw his…" JD's voice trailed off. His jaw steeled. "I didn't like it," he murmured, "I became jealous."

Her eyes widened, surprised that he felt that way at all. Surprised too that he'd admitted to it. And why, she wondered, was he jealous in the first place? She would have thought, given the circumstances, that JD would have enjoyed embarrassing her in front of someone else. The man was an enigma she wasn't likely to figure out any time soon. "Thank you for answering the question," she mumbled, looking away, confused.

"You're welcome."

She cleared her throat. "I'm sorry," she muttered dumbly, not sure of what else to say, "for making you jealous. May I get dressed now?"

"No."

Her head whipped around to look at him.

He settled into his seat and brought the brandy up to his lips. "As a matter of fact remove the blanket again. I was enjoying the view," he said boldly.

She rubbed her temples. "JD…"

"Yes?"

"This is a bit much all at once," she whispered. "Three hours ago I was still officially dating Donald Carver. A blink of an eye later I'm married to you. I think—"

"Did you love Don Carver?" he asked softly.

No, she hadn't, but that was beside the point. She and Don had only been dating two weeks—hardly enough time to fall in love. "Well…"

His eyebrows shot up. "Don't make me jealous again, please."

Candy's heart felt as though it might beat out of her chest. The ice in his voice put her nerves on edge even more so that they already were. He was jealous of Don?

"Take off the blanket," JD reiterated, frowning. "Now."

She shook her head slightly, feeling dazed, more confused by his confessions of jealousy than she cared to be. Taking a calming breath, she quickly discarded the blanket and shoved it back in the cabinet. She fell into her chair as soon as she was done, primly crossing her legs to shield herself as much as possible.

"Open them."

She stilled. "JD please," she murmured. "I'm not used to...to...this."

"Open them," he said again, though more gently this time. His voice was thick again, the arousal that laced his words obvious.

She closed her eyes briefly, then slowly opened her thighs. She could have sworn she heard him suck in his breath again, but was far too nervous to look at his face to verify the supposition.

Candy sat there for another fifteen minutes, her naked flesh on display for her husband, her high heel clad feet dangling from the arms of the chair. His intense blue gaze never seemed to stray from her center. He simply sat there and sipped from his brandy, his eyes memorizing a part of her she would have preferred to keep concealed. She rightly assumed that he was enjoying his arousal, not at all in a hurry to do anything but look. Eventually, however, his need took over.

"Suck on me," he said thickly. "Kneel before me and suck on my cock."

Her head shot up. Her eyes rounded as she swallowed past the lump in her throat.

Candy hesitated, feeling very unsure of herself. Glancing up at his face, she noted that his eyes were narrowed and heavy-lidded. She nibbled on her bottom lip as she watched him unzip his trousers and take out his erection again, his stiff penis now as unconfined as it had been before Tom knocked on the cabin door.

The sight of his arousal gave her frantic mind one less fear—namely that he wanted her to perform on him only so he could make fun of her inability to get him hard. She mentally conceded that the thought had probably been a dumb one considering the fact that he'd been erect for most of the flight, but the thought had occurred to her nevertheless.

JD definitely wanted her. She had no idea why, but realized without a doubt that he did.

She closed her legs and stood up. Slowly coming down on her knees before him, blonde curls cascaded down her back as she took him into her mouth without ceremony. The sound of his breath catching in the back of his throat made those unwanted butterflies flutter in her belly again.

"Very good, sweetheart," JD said hoarsely, his fingers twining through her hair. "Now spend some time getting to know him."

His words were arousing, though she couldn't say why. Because of the thick way he'd uttered them? Because of the way he talked about his erection like it was an entity almost separate from him? She didn't know. All she knew was that her own breathing was quickly growing labored.

She did as he requested, taking his penis in slowly, lingeringly. Candy had given head before—she was over thirty for goodness sake, but it had always been with the intent of arousing the man for intercourse. This was the first occasion she had ever taken her time, licking up and down, familiarizing herself with everything from the puffy vein that ran the length of the shaft to the tiny hole at the tip of the head.

JD cradled her face between his palms the entire time, simply watching her become familiar with his cock, his eyes narrowed and his breathing harsh. He didn't try to coerce her into going faster, so she explored him at her leisure, which he seemed to like anyway.

Candy took his shaft all the way in to the back of her throat, her nipples hardening at the sound of his hiss. Her hands came up to massage his balls, inducing his fingers to tighten their hold on her ringlets.

"I'm going to fuck your face now," he ground out. "I can't take any more toying, sweetheart."

JD rose from his seat, careful not to unlatch her lips from his swollen cock in the process. He held her by the back of the head and gently pushed into her mouth as deeply as he could go, groaning when he felt her lips against his balls.

"That's it," he said hoarsely, his muscles tense as he began to sink his stiff penis in and out of her mouth. "Take all of me."

Before she thought better of it, Candy moaned from around his cock, which she could tell only further inflamed him. He began to ride her mouth faster, his steely buttocks clenching and contracting as he fucked her face.

"Deeper," he hissed. He plunged in and out of her deeper and harder, the sound of saliva and lips meeting steel-hard flesh permeating the cabin. Candy groaned from around his penis then took over the lead. She repeatedly took him all the way to the back of her throat, faster and faster, her head bobbing back and forth as she sucked him off.

His muscles tensed and his breathing grew labored. "I'm going to give you my cum," he gritted out. His hips pistoned back and forth, meeting her every head bob. "Drink it," he said hoarsely.

She took him in all the way, gluttonously pushing the head of his cock to the back of her throat in deep, expert movements. She moaned from around his swollen penis, enjoying the power she felt when his fingers further tightened in her hair and he began to moan uncontrollably.

"Drink it," he groaned, his entire body shuddering. "Drink it all up."

JD came on a bellow, the masculine growl reverberating throughout the airplane's cabin. Her head kept up its steady bobbing motion, her lips extracting every drop of cum he had to give. She was relentless with her sucking, keeping up the feverish pace until he was completely drained, his body spent and satiated.

He collapsed into his seat when he could no longer stand, his breathing ragged. He stared at her for a solid minute, saying nothing, his blue eyes narrowed and his chest heaving. "Suck on my balls," he finally said when his heart rate came down a bit. He cradled her face once again, pushing it into his lap. "It relaxes me."

Candy did, though it didn't have the effect he had said. Either that or they had different ideas of relaxation. Within minutes, his penis was stiff and swollen, ready again to be sucked on. She gave him what he wanted, sucking him off once more before he collapsed altogether and fell asleep.

She stayed kneeled at his feet as he slept, too dazed to move, so completely shell-shocked that not even her sore jaw registered as significant. Thankfully JD slept rather peacefully throughout the rest of the plane ride to the private island, because she didn't feel up to talking—or moving. Once he woke up as if afraid she had left him, but immediately fell back to sleep when he saw that she was still on her knees, still seated before him.

She couldn't have moved if her life depended on it, but then he didn't know that. He had no idea how tumultuous her current thoughts and feelings were.

Given the circumstances, she knew she should have hated him. She had every right to loathe him. Candy told herself over and over again that if she had any self-respect whatsoever left, she wouldn't have enjoyed doing what she had just done to him as much as she had. In fact, she wouldn't have enjoyed it at all.

She blinked, coming out of her trance-like state when it was announced that the plane was about to land. She stood up and quickly dressed herself, wanting the distance of clothing between them before he awoke.

Candy's nostrils flared as she pulled up her skirt. She consoled her injured ego with the knowledge that she hadn't been given a choice in the matter of today's events.

Anything to keep herself from having to deal with the reality that she was as attracted to JD Mahoney as badly as, for whatever reason, he was attracted to her.

Chapter 3

JD's private oasis was even more beautiful than Candy had imagined it would be. Lush palm trees were everywhere, surrounded by gorgeous foliage in varying colors. The sound of exotic birds and beasts punctured the air as servants scurried around to see to the upkeep of the grounds.

The Mahoney estate was even grander than *Chez Ma Coeur*, the large private oasis in the Virgin Islands that had been in the Morgan dynasty for almost a century. JD's island home was palatial in size, the pink marble architecture a perfect example of Spanish influence.

Candy supposed she should have been embarrassed by her constant nudity in front of JD, or at least more so than what she was. Oddly enough, the embarrassment was no longer there. She was still, however, angry. JD had insisted that she take her clothes back off after the plane had landed, so she had been naked during the entire limo ride from the airstrip to the estate.

Her teeth gritted at the perceived insult. When she had signed on the dotted line, she'd had no idea that his revenge would extend to humiliation.

Then again, she hadn't come into contact with anyone else so she couldn't exactly label it humiliation — yet. She'd spotted a few servants when the car had first rolled onto the estate grounds, but they couldn't see her through the tinted limo windows. Still, the very idea that someone *might* see her before all was said and done had left her seething.

Five hours later, she had grown rather accustomed to her lack of attire. And to her blushes. She had even managed to quit seething…somewhat. But bathing him? Her nostrils flared. She was beginning to feel like a slave.

"Soap up my balls," JD arrogantly ordered her. His gaze settled on her nipples. He grazed one with the pad of his thumb, then flicked it with his forefinger. "You'll be sucking on them quite often so use something you don't mind the taste of."

Candy's face went scorching red. "Yes, sir," she gritted out as she quickly saturated his scrotum with coconut oil and just as quickly rubbed it in.

JD closed his eyes as he reclined back in the large, ornate tub that resembled a small wading pool. He rested his head on a bathing pillow, his arms leisurely slung over his head.

Either he hadn't noticed her irritation or he was purposely ignoring it, she thought glumly. Damn it! Didn't anything get to the man? She just prayed he would tire of this "honeymoon" at some point sooner than two months. She needed to get back to Atlanta — and to finding a way to reverse the take-over.

Knee-deep in water, Candy washed JD from head to toe, scrubbing his skin as best as she could with her hands. He hadn't permitted her to use a washcloth on him, so she was forced to clean him like this, her hands that were filled up with lathered soap running up and down his muscular chest, torso, and legs. She carefully avoided his swollen penis, thinking some things were better off left undisturbed.

She frowned as she studied his body. If anything, she begrudgingly admitted, he had only gotten better with age. The body that had once been athletically but boyishly lean was now heavy with muscle. The face that had once been boyishly handsome was now defined, sleek, and matured. She glanced away, distressed by the direction her thoughts had been going in. *He hates you, idiot. Do try to remember that…*

"Touch him," JD's hoarse voice murmured to her.

Candy glanced up. She nibbled on her lower lip, realizing at once what "him" he was talking about. Her amber gaze trailed down the length of his body, zeroing in on the large erection jutting out of the water.

"Touch him," he said thickly, his intense blue eyes slowly opening to regard her.

His eyelids were heavy, the timbre to his voice indicating arousal. His nipples, once flat, had knotted into tiny, tight beads.

Candy blew out a breath. His arousal was inducing her own. Surprise, surprise, she thought grimly.

There was something else too. Something more than arousal feeding arousal. There was also the knowledge that, regardless to the circumstances of their marriage, ordinary old Candy Morgan had made the beautiful, powerful JD Mahoney as hard as a rock. Again and again.

Her hand came out slowly, inching its way down his long body. She felt his stomach muscles clench as her fingers brushed through his dark pubic hair, then down lower to cup his balls.

"The shaft," he said thickly. "Touch the shaft."

She gently squeezed his balls and released them, making him hiss. Encouraged, she wrapped her hand around his thick penis, and slowly began to masturbate him. She could hear his breathing grow more and more labored as her hand glided up and down the length of him.

"Harder," he gritted out. "Faster."

She pumped his cock fast, squeezing it hard as she did so. She would have thought such a squeeze would put a man in agony, but conversely, it had just the opposite effect. He was moaning within seconds, his head falling back down to rest against the pillow, his chest heaving.

"Do you like that?" she murmured, feeling unexpectedly bold. She pumped him harder, faster. Her free hand ran over his chest, feeling the muscles beneath her palm.

"I love it," he said hoarsely. He half-heartedly batted at her hand. "Stop, sweetheart. Stop before I come."

But for some perverse reason she was enjoying this power over him. She didn't obey, deciding to pump his penis harder and faster.

"Oh Candy," he groaned, his jaw clenching. His toes curled as she kept up the relentless pumping.

He gave up, his head falling back yet again to rest on the bathing pillow. He closed his eyes and enjoyed the sensual assault, moaning and groaning as she vigorously masturbated him. She kept up the pace for a solid two minutes, watching with more awe than she wanted to feel as he climbed closer and closer toward orgasm.

His muscles tensed, telling her the moment was almost at hand. His teeth gritted, underlining that fact. But just as she knew he was about to come, his hand firmly grabbed hers, stopping her.

"I will not," he panted out, "waste my cum. I want every drop in your body."

Par for the course, his words further aroused her, the image of him coming inside of her there between them. She stood up, suddenly feeling awkward. "I—I better get you a towel," she hedged, glancing away from him, uncertain how she should feel about the undeniable attraction she felt towards her unwanted husband. "I'll, uh, be right back."

She quickly scurried from the large pool-like tub, her naked buttocks visible to him as she made her way towards the towel rack. She stood before the rack as if in a daze, her thoughts and emotions at war.

She wanted him. She didn't want him.

She loved him. She hated him.

No, she thought, her eyes briefly closing. That wasn't precisely right. She didn't hate him—he hated her.

Candy gasped when she felt his warm, wet hands cup her buttocks from behind and squeeze them. She hadn't heard him emerge from the bathing pool.

"I've always loved your ass," JD said thickly, surprising her, as he shifted his hips so she could feel his aroused penis poking at the flesh of her behind.

Her eyes rounded as he placed the tip at the hole of her anus. "I—I didn't know you'd ever noticed it before," she breathed out.

"Oh I've noticed it all right," he murmured. He rotated his hips, his stiff cock again poking at the entrance to her anus. "You've got a great ass."

Her breathing grew labored. She was torn between fear of the unknown and arousal that had been induced from the knowledge that he liked this part of her body. Conflicted, she offered him no resistance when he nudged her body down so that she was bent over the towel rack.

"So round and so sweet. And so...virgin."

She swallowed roughly. That much was true. "I—I've never had a man there," she said a bit shakily, confirming his suspicions.

That only turned him on more. "Good," he said thickly, one of his hands snaking around her front to find her clit. "I don't like the idea of another man fucking you—anywhere." He rubbed her clit in a circular motion, massaging it as she gasped. "You're so sexy," he purred against her ear, further pressing his erection against her anus. "The sexiest woman I've ever laid eyes on."

Her eyes rounded at the compliment, then bulged when she felt the firm pressure produced by the tip of his cock slipping into her ass. "JD," she said in a frightened voice. She moaned when his fingers rubbed her clit faster, her head falling down to rest on the towel rack.

"I put coconut oil on him," he said hoarsely, his voice kept to a whisper. "Once we get the whole head in, you'll be fine, sweetheart."

He rubbed her clit harder, making her body involuntarily buck against his as she moaned. The head slipped all the way into her asshole, inducing her eyes to fly open. She tensed up on him, her body rigid.

JD rubbed her clit mercilessly, to the point where Candy could do nothing but moan loudly as he brought her quickly toward orgasm. *"JD,"* she groaned, her body bucking up against his again. *"Oh my God."*

Candy cried out as she burst, the orgasm powerful and violent. He sank his cock into her asshole at the same time she orgasmed, seating himself to the hilt. She gasped again, her eyes wide with shock.

"I'm all the way in," he thickly announced, standing still, giving her time to adjust. "You did it. You're fine," he said softly, encouragingly.

She swallowed roughly, but nodded. He was right. Getting past the head had been the difficult part.

His hips slowly began to undulate, back and forth, ever so slowly. The fingers of one hand dug into her hip while the fingers of the other hand continued to massage her drenched, shaved pussy. She gasped, the feeling, as always, arousing in the extreme.

He picked up the pace a bit as he sank in and out of her, his moans filling the bathing chamber. "Oh Christ," he gritted out, his voice so hoarse he sounded as though he was being tortured to death. His cock plunged in and out of her pliable flesh, able to go faster and deeper now that her body had adjusted to the size of him. "You're so tight, sweetheart. My God, you're so fucking tight…"

Candy threw her hips back at him, enjoying the way he was fucking her ass now that she could take it. It was an odd feeling, but an undeniably arousing one. Coupled with the clit massage it was driving her over the edge.

She moaned as she met his thrusts, her breasts jiggling beneath her as her husband's hand massaged her clit and his cock impaled her asshole. *"I'm coming,"* she wailed, her oncoming orgasm so powerful it made her feel hysterical. *"Oh my God – JD."*

She came loudly and violently, her entire body acutely sensitive as an orgasm ripped through her belly. She screamed at the intensity of it, hysterical sounds bubbling up from her throat as he repeatedly sank into her.

He groaned as if in agony, massaging her wet pussy in fast, circular strokes while he fucked her ass harder. He pumped her for another solid minute, his moans filling up the bathing chamber.

"I'm coming too," JD panted, unable to last as long as he wanted to inside such a tight hole. His hips pistoned back and forth, his body animalistically pounded into hers.

She could hear his breathing growing labored, short puffs of breath warming her ear. "Oh fuck – *Candy*."

He bellowed out her name as he came, his entire body shuddering over hers. He moaned as she continued to throw her hips back at him, her tight anus extracting every drop of cum his body had to give.

"Candy," he groaned again, though weaker this time.

His fingers dug into the flesh of her hips as their undulations began to wane. "Candy," he said softly. "Thank you."

Candy closed her eyes as the undulations ceased, unsure of what to say, unsure of what to feel.

James Douglas Mahoney III had just taken her up the ass, she thought, dazed. She didn't know whether to laugh, whether to cry, whether to scream, or whether to thank the gods that she had finally felt the object of her longtime desire sink his cock inside of her body. As always where JD was concerned, her emotions were in chaos. She'd loved him half of her life, yet she hated him for what he'd done to her and Morgan Chemicals.

"You're welcome," she whispered, for some reason wanting the intimacy between them to last. It was a moment of truce, she realized.

While they were joined like this, they were simply a man and a woman, two lovers basking in the aftermath of sex.

Instead of two enemies, each of them plotting to conquer the other.

JD kept uncharacteristically quiet, as if he too recognized the poignancy of the moment. Wordlessly, and tenderly, he pulled out of her body and carried her back to the bath.

Candy didn't meet his gaze the entire time he bathed her. Why was he being so gentle with her? she wondered as his hands massaged soap onto her breasts. She decided not to question his motivations and to simply enjoy the moment.

Still, she wished it could always be like this, she conceded. Not necessarily sexual per se, but calm. She wished she could erase the past and make it go away for good. Would Lawrence's faithlessness haunt their lives forever?

She sighed as she resignedly accepted the fact that it just might.

Chapter 4

"I can't believe you still won't let me put on my clothes," Candy hissed. She absently frowned down at the dinner plate that had been set before her, then glanced around the room they were seated in. The dining parlor was huge and airy, the architecture Spanish to match the rest of the estate's tropical theme.

This was the third day they'd been on the island and she still hadn't seen a stitch of clothing. Or another person, though she knew others were here. The good humor she'd been entertaining toward her husband on their wedding night had long since dissolved, replaced with irritation. "If I had known that I was going to be treated in this fashion…"

"What would you have done?" JD murmured, his penetrating gaze meeting hers.

Her nostrils flared. She still would have married him and they both knew it. It was either this or watch in helplessness as her unskilled mother and brother were tossed out onto the streets. "I hope you're enjoying yourself—"

"Immensely."

"—Because it won't last forever."

His eyebrows rose. "You don't intend on keeping your part of the bargain?" He raised a glass of Pinot Grigio to his lips. "How unsporting of you, sweetheart."

"I'm going to find a way to get Morgan Chemicals back," she gritted out. "Just you watch me."

Silence.

Candy idly wondered why she'd been at his throat all day long. Her nudity hadn't bothered her on the first or second day of their honeymoon, so why now?

She frowned, refusing to accept the possibility that she was feeling rejected by the fact that he hadn't made a move to consummate their marriage as of yet. Indeed, he hadn't touched her since the night he took her anal virginity — and now she felt foolish for having entertained such romantic notions of him after the deed had been done. Her pride, she conceded, was smarting at the perceived rejection.

There was also the undeniable fact that this man had stolen her company, her livelihood, and her pride in one fell swoop. When he wasn't touching her or making her touch him, it was easier to concentrate on her anger.

JD set down the glass of white wine and steepled his fingertips. "You have no way of getting the company back and we both know it. Now stop being petulant and eat your fish."

She snorted, rolling her eyes. "Where there's a will there's a way. And I'm allergic to fish."

He hadn't seemed worried in the least about her threats, yet oddly enough, the fish comment got to him. "I'm sorry, sweetheart. I didn't know that. I'll order you something else."

Her hand whipped out and came to rest on his. "Please don't ring the bell," she said quietly. "I'd rather eat the fish than have someone see me naked."

She thought she saw something gentle in his eyes, but she couldn't be sure. She slowly removed her hand and glanced away.

"Did you have something to do with it?" he asked softly, throwing her off guard.

Candy blinked. Her forehead wrinkled as she looked at him. "Something to do with what?"

"With getting me fired all those years ago." His jaw tightened. "With stealing my ideas and passing them off to the board as Lawrence's."

She sighed. "JD...I feel awful about what my father did, but—"

"Just answer the question," he murmured. "A simple yes or no will suffice."

She looked him dead in the eye. "No," she said firmly. "I didn't know you were fired until a week after it happened. It was another two months before I found out what he'd done to you." Her back straightened. "You may not believe me, because I am in fact a Morgan, but it's the truth."

Silence.

JD picked up his wineglass and sipped from it. "If you felt so badly," he asked, his voice deceptively unemotional, "then why didn't you help me?" He waved a hand. "Lawrence would have done anything you asked and everyone knew it."

"That's not true," she whispered. She cleared her throat and glanced away. She had pleaded with her father to hire JD back until her voice was raw...all to no avail. "I don't know where you got your misinformation, but Lawrence only doted on the people he could control. I wasn't one of them. Neither were you."

"Touché."

"He left me everything in his will, that's true, but it wasn't out of love I can assure you."

"The lesser of three evils? In his eyes, I mean?"

She shrugged, though the gesture was far from nonchalant. She had wanted Lawrence to love her. It still pained her that he never had. He might have been corrupt, but he was still her father. "Something like that," she whispered.

More silence.

"You may wear clothing whenever it's likely that the servants will be around, but I want you naked at all times when it's just us."

She glanced up, her eyes round. She hadn't been expecting that concession. "You believe me then?" she asked quietly.

He sighed. "I might be a goddamn fool, but yes, I believe you."

"So you're not going to punish me any longer?"

His brow furrowed. "Punish you?"

She waved a hand. "By forcing me to be nude in front of the entire world."

He looked at her quizzically. "That was never a punishment."

She snorted at that. "Then why did you do it? To make me a better person?" she asked sarcastically.

He shrugged. "I prefer you naked." His eyes hardened. "And it wasn't the entire world. It was only me. I've made certain nobody else has seen you, so quit being so dramatic."

Candy sighed, knowing he was right. Still, there had been a few close calls. Close enough, at any rate, to make her blood run cold. Yet now he was telling her there would be no more close calls either. He was almost being, well...nice.

She rubbed her temples, deciding that she wasn't likely to solve the riddle of James Douglas Mahoney III tonight. And, quite frankly, she was too exhausted to try. "Fine. May I have my clothes now?"

"No."

She threw him an exasperated look. "But you just said—"

"I said that when we are alone you will always be naked." He looked around the dining parlor for effect. "We are, in fact, alone."

Her teeth gritted. "A technicality. A servant could walk in at any time!"

"Not without my permission. They know better."

"What if there was a kitchen fire and they all came running in here?"

He rolled his eyes.

"Or what if, I don't know, a hurricane was on its way to the island and they ran in here to warn you? Or what if—"

"I think you're forgetting about Clauses 52 and 53 of our prenuptial agreement," he interrupted.

Her eyes narrowed. "What were Clauses 52 and 53? There were so many damn clauses it's hard to keep them all straight!"

"I can provide you with a photo-static copy if you'd like."

"...Arrg!"

"Clause 52," he continued on undaunted, "states that my wife shall do what I tell her *without question* at all times. Clause 53 states that my wife shall remain sweet-tempered, agreeable, and biddable to me at all times." His eyebrows rose. "You've broken two Clauses in two minutes time. Not a good start, darling. And on our honeymoon no less. Tsk. Tsk."

Her nostrils flared. "That prenuptial agreement is ridiculous and we both know it!"

He rose from his chair and threw the napkin in his hand onto the table. "To you, perhaps, but not to me."

Candy rubbed her temples, the fight going out of her. "Where are you going?" she asked weakly. Her lips pinched together. "And if putting a question to you breaks one of your dumb Clauses I don't want to hear about it!"

"To get you something to eat," he said with exaggerated patience. "You can't eat fish, you don't want Marcel in here, so I'm going to fetch you some dinner myself."

"Oh." There wasn't much in the way of bitchy she could say to that.

True to his word, he fetched her a plate filled with fruit, assorted cheeses, bread, and a hunk of chocolate cake. They spent the remainder of the meal in silence, both of them lost in their own thoughts.

When it was over, JD escorted her to their third floor bedroom using a back entrance so nobody would see her nude body. He drew her into his arms after closing the door behind them and kissed her passionately. His hands caressed her breasts, her ass, her vagina, her everything, as his lips devoured her mouth. By the time he raised his head and drew away from her, she was breathless and panting.

"I'll see you tomorrow," he murmured, his hand settling possessively at one breast. He rubbed the nipple with the pad of his thumb. "I'm giving you a little more time to get used to the idea of being owned by me, so I suggest you use it wisely." His eyes roamed from her face down to her shaved mons and back again. "I'm not an overly patient man."

Candy nodded, wide-eyed, a depraved sense of disappointment settling in. She watched JD leave through the bedroom's double doors, half of her glad to see him go, the other half wanting him to come back.

She sank down into the lush pillowing of the bed, a sigh escaping from her lips. Climbing between the sheets, she reached over and turned off the bedside lamp, then curled up alone in the big bed.

Why had JD married her? she asked herself for what felt to be the millionth time. What was it that he wanted from her? He kept talking about rigid ownership and equally rigid marriage clauses, yet for all his bluster his actual actions toward her thus far had been far gentler, almost even understanding at times. It was as if he wanted her to want him back.

Candy rolled over onto her side, telling herself it was best if she got some sleep and tried to forget about her enigmatic husband. Tomorrow would come soon enough. And with it hopefully some real answers.

* * * * *

JD had known that Candy would see things his way given time. He had been right. Lawrence Morgan's daughter was everything the old bastard had touted her to be and then some. She was the rock that had kept the corrupt patriarch's family together all of these years. She was the brains of the company and had, in fact, managed to divert three of JD's previous attempts to take over Morgan Chemicals.

The takeover had, in the end, been inevitable. JD had been patient on each of the previous occasions that Candy had managed to thwart him. He'd known that Lawrence had all but squandered the company's assets before his death, which meant that there was only so much salvaging little Candy could do.

Again, he had been right. Finally — *finally* — the sins of Lawrence Morgan had come full circle. And James

Douglas Mahoney III would get the inheritance he had been promised long ago by Lawrence's lying lips.

He would get the beautiful, practical, Candace Marie Morgan. He would get the woman he'd been taunted and teased with all of the years he'd worked for Lawrence. He would get the same up-on-a-pedestal woman who had seemed so out of reach and unattainable to a man who had heralded from a working class background of meager means.

"She sure is a treasure," Lawrence gloated as the two men watched Candy work at her desk. She didn't know that she was being watched. "Oh sure, she's not much to look at, but she's smart as a whip and loyal to the bone."

JD's forehead wrinkled. How could he think she wasn't much to look at? She didn't resemble the anorexic mistresses Lawrence always had hanging around the office clamoring for his attention (and wallet), but he'd never seen a more exotic, lush beauty. Personally, JD preferred her voluptuous curves to the small-chested, skinny women Lawrence cheated on his wife with. "I agree," JD murmured, "that she is a treasure."

Lawrence smiled. "I'm glad you feel that way. Because I mean to give her to you, son."

His eyebrows rose. "Give her to me?"

Lawrence snorted at his confusion. "I know it's not politically correct to talk about a woman in such a way, but believe me, son, marriages of the wealthy are always arranged. Generally not put in those terms, but it amounts to the same thing. A man can't afford for his heiress to go to just anyone."

"Heiress? Won't your son be inheriting?"

"Not a dime."

Looking back, JD should have seen that as his first sign of what Lawrence was truly like. How any man could cut off his own son without a qualm was beyond his fathoming capabilities. But he had looked up to the older man, had even managed to overlook his in-your-face infidelities as a sign of weakness, because Lawrence Morgan had gone out of his way to make JD believe that he was destined to be someone. It didn't matter that his beginnings were humble, Lawrence had convinced him. Might made right. And James Douglas Mahoney III had all of the fortitude and drive to reach greatness.

His eyes blazed as he watched Candy work. The unattainable daughter of Lawrence Morgan had all but been offered to him on a silver platter. To a man who had been born the son of a janitor and a waitress, it seemed too good to be true.

She looked so sweet and innocent sitting there, with her long blond curls framing her cherub's face. She resembled a lamb that had no knowledge it was about to be consumed by a lion. But right now she was only eighteen, he reminded himself, and working at Morgan Chemicals part time while she earned her university degree. Lawrence would give her a few more years to mature and then he would ask JD to take her hand in marriage.

"I'd be honored to marry your daughter," JD said in low tones, his gaze mesmerized by the sight of her. "Very honored…"

JD had idealized Candy all of these years, he realized. He'd placed her on a pedestal that no other woman had ever been able to reach and because of it his relationships invariably ended when the women in his life fell short by comparison.

Two years later when Lawrence had given JD the boot, it hadn't been his lost job that he'd mourned. It hadn't even been the stolen project that he hadn't been credited for, a project that had raked in millions for Morgan Chemicals. It had been the loss of Candy that had made him vicious and more dangerous than he'd ever been. She had been dangled before him like a mirage in the desert, then snatched away without remorse.

The sins of Lawrence Morgan have come full circle…

JD threw his tie down on the nightstand, preparing to go to bed—tonight and only tonight without his mirage in the desert. He knew his wife hated him right now. Knew too that despite what he'd said to Candy, he hoped things weren't always strained between them.

He stood before him stunned, vulnerable. He could scarcely believe he'd been fired, that the man he looked up to had stolen his ideas, passed them off as his own, then done away with him without so much as blinking.

And Candy. Oh God…

Lawrence threw his head back and laughed. "You? Marry my daughter?" He shook his head, bemused. "Candy could never stomach an ill-bred thing like you touching her." His gloating smile dissolved into a frown. "Now get the hell out of my office before I have security throw you out."

JD stilled as the memories came crashing back. His nostrils flared. His wife might think him beneath her, but regardless she was his now. She would always be his.

He had won—*won*. He had taken over Morgan Chemicals and Candy had been given no choice but to accept him as her husband. It was either that or her family would lose everything. In truth, he had no intention of taking anything away from her family, but a sharp businessman knew when to use the right card. JD was the sharpest.

And so now Candace Marie Morgan was his. His to fuck, his to breed, his to…own. If it was the only way he could have her, he'd take it.

JD had no intention of settling for a polite, unfamiliar relationship with his wife as so many of the socially elite did. When he had told her that she belonged to him, he had meant it.

Every last word of it.

Chapter 5

"Show me your cunt." His jaw tightened. "Whenever we are alone and sitting down together, I want your legs spread wide apart at all times. I shouldn't have to ask to see something that belongs to me."

The air chilled as evening settled in, inducing her skin to goose pimple. Her nipples hardened as a cool breeze hit them, stiffening them into tight, sensitive peaks. "May I please put my clothes back on?" Candy asked. Reclining on a cabana lounger, she absently glanced down at the untouched margarita sitting before her, then toward the pool that had been built to look like an island lagoon. Surrounding the pool was a faux jungle, thickly laced with palm trees and exotic ferns. "It's getting a bit chilly."

"No," he said simply, glancing up from the computer spreadsheet he had been reading from. His eyes narrowed. "I thought I told you to spread your legs. When I look up from my work I want to see your gorgeous cunt exposed to me." He glanced back down, perusing the paperwork before him.

Her nostrils flared but she spread her legs. "Is this better?" she asked icily.

JD glanced up again. He ignored the perturbed look she was giving him. "Infinitely," he murmured.

Candy sighed, giving up. She had no idea how long he planned to keep her naked and spread eagle, but she hoped the novelty would soon wear off. Besides, she needed time away from him. How else could she plot behind his back to regain her family's empire? Then again, she thought forlornly, he was probably well aware of that fact.

Bastard.

Candy seethed for another ten minutes before she slowly began to drift off to sleep. Her mind was filled with a thousand questions and concerns even as her eyelids grew heavier and heavier, eventually closing altogether.

What did JD want from her? Why did he insist upon keeping her naked and splayed out like this? Was it all about revenge, or was it possible that deep down inside he actually wanted her but refused to admit it?

She fell asleep in the lounger, a cool tropical breeze hitting her exposed flesh, stiffening her nipples. Her last coherent thought was that it really didn't matter what JD's motivations were. The undeniable fact was that he had done exactly what he'd said he was going to do and now he owned her.

* * * * *

"He's so handsome," Candy breathed out, a paper plate filled with a huge piece of chocolate cake clutched to her chest. She bit her lip as she watched JD Mahoney spike the volleyball a final time, thereby winning the game for his team at the Morgan Chemical company picnic. "So handsome," she whispered.

Cheers rang up from the crowd as Candy dreamily studied JD's features. His muscular, athletic body. His chiseled face and gorgeous dark hair. His...

She blushed. She was only sixteen, so she probably shouldn't be looking at him down there.

"You did it!" a feminine voice chirped as a gorgeous, thin redhead threw herself into JD's arms. "You're my hero," she said throatily, her body rubbing up against his aroused one as she kissed him.

Candy closed her eyes, her heart breaking. She didn't want to see JD kiss someone else. She wasn't stupid enough to think that he didn't do those things and then some with the beautiful redhead in private, but at least if she didn't have to see it then she could still pretend...

Candy's brow wrinkled in her sleep. *I can pretend he's mine...all mine.* Her eyes closed tightly, the remembered pain all too real even in slumber.

"Let's get out of here," JD murmured to his female companion. He didn't know that Candy was hiding in the shadows, eavesdropping. "I feel like making love."

Candy's eyes opened. Her heart began beating furiously. Please don't take her home, she thought. Please JD —

"I thought you'd never ask," the redhead purred. "I've been horny for you all afternoon."

He smiled. "Then let's go."

Candy listened as they walked away, emerging from the shadows only when she was certain that the coast was clear. Her head bowed as pain lanced through her, jabbing her in the stomach.

She took a deep breath as she studied the paper plate in her hand. Chocolate cake was her favorite.

Sighing, Candy pitched the plate into a nearby garbage can and headed toward the gates. She didn't want to be here. She didn't feel like eating or playing games or listening to a bunch of boring people make allegedly witty conversation. She just wanted to go home.

She held her head high as she walked through the gates and towards the awaiting limo. She passed by JD and his companion, who were waiting on his car to be brought around, but paid them no attention. She could feel his eyes on her as she hurried past, but pretended obliviousness to his presence as her father's chauffeur opened the limo door for her and she crawled inside.

Only when she was safely at home, after she had locked herself away from the world and prying eyes in the secrecy of her bedroom, did she allow herself to feel emotions again. She crawled between the satin sheets of her plush Cinderella canopy bed and closed her eyes, crying softly as she drifted off to sleep.

Candy awoke abruptly, sadness mingled with an urgent sensation of arousal overpowering her. Still within the clutches of sleep, her mind not fully cognizant of the fact that she had been dreaming, she gasped like a shocked sixteen-year-old when she opened her eyes and saw JD's head buried between her legs.

"JD," she panted, her back arching on the lounger. "What are you — *oh God.*"

She gasped again, her mind now alert to the fact of where she was and what was happening to her. Splayed out naked on the cabana lounger, her nipples stiff and her vagina exposed, her husband was lapping at her pussy, licking it feverishly and nuzzling her clit like a dog that had found a buried bone.

"JD," she breathed out. She threaded her fingers through his hair, pressing his face in closer to her aroused flesh. *"Yes,"* she hissed. She became lost in sensation, lost in emotion, as the sixteen-year-old naïve girl mentally warred with the thirty-year-old mature woman.

JD's lips latched around her clit as he began to mercilessly suck on it. The sound of him slurping her flesh into his mouth rose to her ears. She moaned as her head fell back, her nipples pointing straight up into the crisp evening air. There was no more battle to be fought.

"Harder," she begged. "Suck on it harder."

He readily complied, a barely detectable growl eliciting from the back of his throat as he buried his face between her legs as far as it could humanly go. He sucked harder on her clit, his fingers digging into the flesh of her thighs, holding her body steady as it began to convulse.

Candy came on a loud groan, her entire body shaking as an orgasm ripped through her. Blood rushed up to her face, heating it, and then to her nipples, elongating them. *"Oh yes,"* she moaned, her head thrashing back and forth. *"Oh God."*

Her clit became extraordinarily sensitive, causing her to cry out when he continued to suck on it. "No—JD—please...!"

He ignored her verbal plea and sucked even harder, making her scream from a combination of pleasure and pain. Her hips bucked up from beneath him, threatening to force him to release her. His fingers firmly dug into her thighs instead, refusing to give her cunt up.

A dog with a bone, her hysterical mind kept thinking as her head continued to thrash back and forth. He looked exactly like a dog with a bone...

"Oh. My. God."

Candy screamed, her back arching and her legs instinctively wrapping around JD's neck, as another, stronger orgasm tore through her. She moaned as the climax pounded throughout her body, her legs trembling like leaves in a storm. *"Yes,"* she moaned, her nipples so stiff they ached. *"Yes."*

JD gently unwrapped her legs from around his neck and repositioned them so that they were splayed out on the cushioned arms of the expensive cabana lounger. His face emerged from between her thighs, his eyes intense, as he watched Candy's panting body come down from its high.

When it was over, when she felt calmed and drugged by climax, she looked up, her eyes searching his. Candy took a deep breath, watching as his gaze flicked up from her exposed, shaved mons to her face. Wordlessly, he stood up a moment later and began to shed his suit.

"Your pussy is delicious," he murmured. "As tasty as I always thought it would be."

Her eyes widened. As tasty as he'd always thought it would be? That almost sounded like —

Had he fantasized about her before?

"But now it's time to move onto the next phase," he growled as he unzipped his trousers. "The phase where I fuck you day and night, filling up your cunt with my sperm." One arrogant eyebrow rose as he stepped out of his boxer shorts. "The phase where I get my wife pregnant."

Candy wet her lips. Would he want to get her pregnant if his sole motivation was to get back at her father? Somehow she couldn't see JD Mahoney doing that to a child, but she had to concede that she didn't yet understand him well enough to judge. She experienced a moment's hesitation, uncertain what to do. She was not on the pill, so his desire could very well come true.

"Keep your legs spread wide," JD ordered as he came down on his knees to settle himself between them. "If it were possible, I'd want them that way day and night, your cunt always visible and ready to be fucked by me."

Candy blew out a breath, her arousal growing in leaps and bounds. Some women would find such guttural words a turn-off, but she wasn't one of them. JD personified masculinity with his brash, unschooled ways. He was earthy and rugged — the very things that had first attracted her to him all those years back. It was getting more and more difficult to separate then from now, the sixteen-year-old from the thirty-year-old.

JD ran a possessive hand over her waxed, silky pubic area. "I've never seen a more perfect pussy," he announced in an almost absent fashion. Almost because there was nothing absent about James Douglas Mahoney

III. "It belongs in a magazine." That eyebrow of his rose again. "Except I don't share."

Candy's breathing momentarily stilled. Why was he talking to her this way? Why was he praising her body? And why did he persist in trying to make her feel sexy?

JD palmed his erection, then guided it toward her opening. "I've waited a long, long time to make love to you Candy Marie," he murmured as he covered her body with his. "Too damned long."

Her amber eyes widened a bit at the revelation.

"I wanted to wait until we got to our bedroom," he said hoarsely, his erection poised at her hole, "but I can't."

Candy wet her lips, the confession giving her more courage than she wanted it to. "Then don't," she whispered, feeling emboldened. "I've fantasized about you since I was a teenage girl. Make it real."

His entire body stilled, the muscles tense. "Candy…"

"It's true," she said, blushing. She glanced away. "Please don't make me regret that I confessed it," she whispered.

He was still for a moment, as if working things out in his mind. She wanted to look at him to see his reaction, but was too embarrassed to.

A moment later she was gasping as he plunged into her. He sank into her flesh on a groan, seating his cock to the hilt. He slowly began to rock in and out of her, the sound of her vagina enveloping his stiff penis heightening her arousal.

His jaw was tense, his teeth gritted. "Is this real enough for you, Candy Marie?" he thickly asked.

"Yes," she moaned, her neck baring to him as she arched her back. *"Yes."*

He rotated his hips and pounded into her harder—faster. She gasped, throwing her hips back at him.

"Your cunt feels so good," he said hoarsely, his eyelids heavy.

He palmed her breasts and buried his face between them, feverishly sucking on each nipple as he slammed into her body again and again. The sound of flesh slapping against flesh competed with the sound of her nipples popping out of his mouth as he repeatedly took turns sucking on them.

Candy gasped, a groan escaping from between her lips. She reached down and palmed his buttocks, her fingers digging into the steely mounds. "So good," she murmured, her eyes closed as a tropical breeze washed over their heated bodies. "So good."

"And so mine," JD said possessively as his face rose from her nipples. He released her breasts and twined a long, thick lock of her blonde hair around his hand. His nostrils flaring, he rotated his hips again then slammed his cock into her, his hips surging back and forth as he pounded in and out of her.

"*Oh God*," Candy groaned. Her head began to undulate back and forth as the sound of her pussy enveloping his cock reached her ears. "*Harder*," she begged.

Releasing his hold on her hair, he didn't stop pumping her as he quickly came up to his knees and threw her legs over his shoulders, impaling her again without missing a beat. JD took her impossibly harder, his well-honed body able to withstand the violent pace.

Candy gasped, now able to feel every inch of his long penis buried deep inside of her. She opened her eyes as he mounted her, watching as his thick cock disappeared into her wet flesh with a suctioning sound. Over and over. Again and again. He took her harder and faster and—

"Oh my God." Candy screamed out the words as her eyes closed and her head fell back against the cabana lounger. Her nipples stabbed up into the air and her legs shook from atop his shoulders as her body convulsed in orgasm. *"Yes – oh God JD."*

JD growled as he fucked her, the sound of his name on her lips as she came making him go wild. His fingers dug into the flesh of her thighs as he mercilessly pounded into her, mating her like an animal. "You're mine," he ground out, his muscles slick and corded as he buried himself in her pussy over and over, again and again. *"Mine."*

He came down on top of her, covering her body with his larger one as her legs instinctively wrapped around his hips. His palms cupped her breasts as he surged in and out of her, relentlessly branding her with his cock as his hands possessively held onto her breasts.

His face looked pained, as if he knew he was about to come and didn't want to – as if he wanted the moment to last forever.

JD plunged into her pussy to the hilt, riding her with hard, deep strokes. His eyes closed, his muscles tense, he sank into her flesh once, twice, three times more.

"Candy."

He came on a loud groan, his jaw clenched as his cum spurted deep inside of her, his rigid body shuddering atop hers. He held onto her tightly, bit by bit coming down in pace, until finally he'd been depleted.

When their marriage had been fully consummated, neither of them moved a muscle nor spoke a word for a long while. They both laid there, replete and exhausted, for what felt like hours.

Candy continued to cling onto JD's body, her arms wrapped around his center. He was still holding onto her too, she noted, and he didn't seem inclined to let go.

Her eyes drifted upwards. Her gaze absently watched the silhouette of a palm tree sway lazily in the nighttime breeze, the crescent-shaped moon behind it providing a mystical ambiance for an evening that left her wishing for things she had no business wanting.

She closed her eyes as she held her husband tightly, her thoughts on what would become of them after this night. Could JD ever forget what Lawrence had done to him? And if he couldn't, would he ever be able to view her as an entity separate from the man who had once taken everything away from him?

Candy sighed as her hands stroked JD's back. Whether they divorced tomorrow or stayed together, she hoped that would be the case and that her husband would see her for herself rather than as an extension of Lawrence. Otherwise, she thought sadly, they had no hope for a friendship let alone anything else.

And her father's sins would have effectively destroyed two more lives.

Chapter 6
Two weeks later

"Why did he do it, do you suppose?"

Candy blinked. She glanced up from the novel she'd been reading, aware of JD's presence for the first time. Lying on a cabana lounger next to the pool, she'd been relaxing while he worked. She was wearing a cotton sundress today, one of many times she'd been clothed these past two weeks.

She squinted her eyes up at him. "Why did who do what?"

He took the seat next to hers, tugging at the knees of his trousers as he sat. "Lawrence. Why do you suppose he would turn on me like that?"

Candy sighed as she snapped the book shut. "You're looking for logic where little exists."

He shrugged, his expression remote. "Perhaps," he murmured.

"You probably frightened him," she admitted. "He saw potential in you he knew he didn't have. Lawrence was infamous for squelching the competition."

"But I wasn't competition. I was on his side."

She stared at his face, her gaze taking in his expression. It occurred to her for the first time since they'd been married that it wasn't simply anger JD had been harboring all of these years. There was also a great deal of hurt. She didn't know why the revelation surprised her, but it did. She tended to think of her husband as superhuman, not in the least bit vulnerable to anyone or anything.

"You loved him," she said softly. "Didn't you?"

JD frowned. "I'm not gay—"

"You know what I mean."

He sighed, glancing away. "I suppose I—yes," he quietly admitted. "I looked up to him, I admired him, I…"

"Loved him."

He smiled a bit sadly. "Like a father," he murmured.

Candy's eyes flicked over his face. "I know how you feel," she whispered. She swallowed against the lump of emotion in her throat, a feeling of connection and camaraderie with her husband forged in that moment. "I loved him too. He didn't love me back."

JD stilled. "I'm sorry he made you feel that way," he said in low tones, his intense blue eyes finding hers, "but I know that Lawrence did love you."

She blew out a breath, looking away.

"In as much as Lawrence Morgan could love another person, he did love you, Candy."

She stared unblinking at the pool. "Why are you saying this to me?" she quietly asked. "I should be the one trying to make amends on my father's behalf to you, not you to me."

She didn't particularly want JD to show her so much caring. It made it more difficult to keep the walls around her heart intact. For the past two weeks he'd been getting under her skin and she didn't particularly want him there.

What if she fell in love with him? Or worse yet, what if she fell in love with him and then he left her? At least if he had their marriage dissolved at this juncture she could still forge onward.

She hoped.

"Because you needed to hear it. And because it's the truth." He stood up, staring at her, briefly hesitating before turning to leave. "I need to get some work done. I'll see you tonight at dinner."

Candy watched him walk away, her stomach muscles clenching. He kept trying to reach out to her, to forge a bond where she didn't want one ever since the evening they'd consummated their marriage. He was getting to her. He was getting to her so badly that it frightened her. Yet in that moment she felt guilty about the fact that she'd attempted to rebuff all of his overtures toward her these past two weeks simply because she was scared.

He was trying to be her friend. He didn't have many friends.

"JD," she softly called out.

He stilled, but didn't turn around to face her.

"Thank you," she whispered.

He was quiet for a long moment. "You're welcome," he murmured.

* * * * *

"Hi."

JD glanced up, his expression a bit startled. Candy supposed she couldn't blame him for his surprise. In the two plus weeks she'd been on the island, this was the first time she had ever actively sought out his company.

"Uh...hi." JD closed the ledger he had been writing notes in and motioned for her to have a seat on the other side of his desk. "What can I help you with?"

Candy smiled. The man didn't know how to be anything less than formal and businesslike. Running a company was all he knew. Being in charge was a way of life. She realized he didn't have many friends, but found herself wondering for the first time if he had any at all.

From what she could gather of his lifestyle, he worked himself to the bone, which would leave little time for social relationships. For executives with easygoing personalities who liked maintaining various superficial acquaintances, such a situation wouldn't prevent them from having a ton of social contacts. But for a man like JD who rarely smiled, was overly serious, and didn't trust others to boot...

"I was thinking," Candy said as she took the seat across from his desk, "that it might be fun if we went to see a movie or something. Maybe go out to eat." She glanced around his island office, having never been inside of it before. It looked about like she'd expected—mostly bare with a few personal items neatly scattered around. "What do you think?"

Those intense eyes of his bore into hers. "You, uh...you want to go out to eat?" He cleared his throat. "With me?"

"Well yeah." She grinned. "Being my husband and all, you seemed the logical choice."

She could have sworn she saw a bit of red stain his cheeks. A fact that made her heart thump pleasurably in her chest.

He blew out a breath. "All right. What movie would you like to see? Where would you like to eat?"

She stretched her hands. "Is there any place on the island to go?"

He frowned as he thought the question over. "No," he said quietly. "No, there isn't. I'm sorry."

If she didn't miss her beat, he looked a bit disappointed. Candy straightened in the chair, still smiling. "That's all right. Why don't we do something else? Maybe we can just skip the movie, take a boat ride to the mainland, and tool around for the day. If you're not too busy, of course."

JD stilled. His gaze flicked over her face, studying it. "I'm not too busy for you," he murmured.

Her heart began to palpitate, dramatically beating in her breast. "Good," she whispered. She cleared her throat. "Good," she said a bit louder. She stood up, nervously ran her palms down the front of her cotton dress, and smiled. "I've never been to Costa Rica. This should be fun."

He was quiet for a long moment, leaving Candy decidedly nervous. She wondered for one horrified moment if she'd read him wrong and that he didn't want to take time away from his work to spend it with her. Her pulse began to drop, her smile to fade.

"I agree," JD murmured as he stood up. His smile came slowly, but when it came it damn near took her breath away with its genuineness and masculine beauty. "I know of a terrific little Spanish restaurant I think you'll enjoy."

Candy took a deep breath and exhaled as he rounded the desk and joined her. She grinned up to him as he threaded his larger fingers through her comparatively smaller ones. "That sounds wonderful."

JD's gaze clashed with hers. She blinked, not recognizing the expression on his face. On any other man she would have called it happiness, perhaps even gratefulness, but on him she just couldn't tell.

He slowly lifted one of her hands, the one that was threaded through his, and raised it to his lips. Her heart began drumming like mad again, her eyes wide, as he gently kissed it.

"Thank you," JD said softly, his eyes tracking her face.

Candy swallowed roughly, a shiver running up and down her spine. "You're welcome," she breathed out.

Chapter 7
One week later

Candy sank down onto her husband's cock, impaling herself in one smooth thrust. She sighed breathily, enjoying the feeling of having her body stuffed full of him.

"Candy," JD said groggily. It was the middle of the night. And the very first time she had ever initiated sex between them. "What are you—oh sweetheart, that feels so good."

She gently smiled as she slowly rode up and down the length of his rock-hard shaft. Her hands came down to massage his chest, her fingers running over his tight male nipples as she made love to him.

JD sucked in his breath. His teeth gritted. "Oh baby—goddamn I love your pussy."

And she loved his cock—and him.

That revelation had woken her up tonight from a peaceful sleep. She loved him. She had always loved him. It didn't matter what had happened in the past. Somehow she would find a way to make things right.

He had become more than a man to her these past few weeks—he had become her best friend too. What's more, she knew she was his best friend as well. She realized that connection meant more to him than anything else. He could marry anyone. He could breed anyone. But he couldn't reach out, wanting to be best friends with just anyone.

Over the past three weeks, JD had come to mean more to her than she'd ever thought possible. In stark contrast to the first few days of their married life, her husband had revealed the gentle, kind side of himself that he apparently reserved for her and her alone.

She'd paid a great deal of attention to how he interacted with others. He was autocratic, domineering, unwilling to compromise — but with her he was somehow different. During the past three weeks she couldn't recall one personal decision he had made without consulting with her first. From what they would eat for breakfast to what stocks she thought he should invest in, he valued her opinion.

Where JD was loud and a bit harsh with others, he was gentle and soft-spoken where she was concerned. He didn't seem too interested in the feelings of very many people, but conversely, her feelings seemed to matter to him more than his own.

She liked that — needed it even. It made her feel special. It made her feel desirable.

It made her feel loved.

"I missed you," she whispered, throwing a lock of blonde ringlets over her shoulder. She smiled down to him as she continued to slowly ride him. "I didn't want to wait until morning."

JD's gaze clashed with hers. He didn't smile, but she saw something gentle in his eyes. "Never apologize," he murmured, his hands finding her hips. "I missed you too, sweetheart."

Their gazes locked and held as they made love. He looked almost vulnerable to her, if such a thing were possible where James Douglas Mahoney III was concerned. Perhaps she was being overly romantic, perhaps what she saw in those murky blue eyes was nothing but fatigue and arousal, but she liked to think that there was more to it than that.

"Kiss me," she whispered. "I need to be closer to you."

Again, that gentling in his eyes. "Come here," he murmured, one strong hand reaching up to bend her head down to meet his. He thrust his tongue inside, meeting hers.

They kissed long and leisurely, the same as they made love. They took their time exploring each other's bodies, neither of them in any rush to stop in the name of sleep.

Candy raised her head and smiled down to him as she ran her fingers through his dark hair. She continued to ride him slowly, her pussy enveloping and re-enveloping his cock over and over, again and again.

This is how it should be, she thought. This is how she wanted it to be. She'd never felt closer to another human being in her entire life.

Candy sighed contentedly as they made love, wishing that this night never had to end.

* * * * *

Candy rustled through the paperwork on the desk in JD's private study, careful to keep quiet so she wouldn't be caught. He had been asleep for over two hours, she reminded herself, and soundly at that. All would be well.

A part of her felt guilty for going behind his back and looking through his things like this, but the other part of her needed answers. She wanted to know what had become of her family since JD hadn't been inclined to discuss them with her. Her thoughts turned to the conversation they'd had last night in their bedroom following dinner.

"There's plenty of time for that," he hedged. *"I don't wish to discuss the Morgan family tonight."*

"But JD – "

"Please," he said quietly, his mesmerizing blue eyes snagging hers. "Not tonight," he murmured. "I'd rather concentrate on getting my heir or heiress in your belly."

"At some point we have to talk," she said, glancing away.

"We talk plenty, don't we? About lots of things." He walked across the room and stood beside her, his hand coming up to gently knead her shoulder.

She bit her lip. "I meant about my family."

He sighed. "I know what you meant. But please, Candy, not tonight…"

He had made love to her then, which hadn't come as any surprise. In fact, JD had taken her so many times over the past three plus weeks that she would be surprised if it turned out she *wasn't* pregnant. On the stairs, in the dining parlor, by the pool, in his office, in their bed, missionary, doggy, woman-on-top, spooning — they'd done it in every way imaginable and in ways she hadn't previously thought possible.

Her husband seemed almost obsessed with her, Candy thought as she rifled through his desk drawers. Like he had plotted for years to have her all to himself and was making the most of the situation now that she was ensnared.

That was probably true. But was his motivation revenge…or something more?

One part of her believed that JD had fallen for her, but the other part kept wondering, kept feeding her doubts. Either way, she needed to know. By finding out what had become of her family, she was pretty certain she would have her answers. After all, if you love a woman and wanted to keep her happy, you could hardly throw her family out on the street.

Candy cursed under her breath when she came to a drawer that was locked. *Stay focused, Candy. You need to find out what happened.* She impatiently glanced around for a key, sighing when she couldn't find one. *He's no fool*, she thought. *All of the answers have to be in this drawer. Why else would he have locked it?*

Her forehead wrinkled as she considered the puzzle before her in a logical fashion. JD wouldn't leave the key in plain sight, she knew, but as busy of a man as he was, she doubted if he kept it far from the desk. He'd want it easily accessible…

She glanced around, her eyes darting back and forth. A photograph of his deceased parents on one wall, an original Picasso on another, a clay urn that looked Egyptian in origin—

Her gaze flew back to the photo of his deceased parents. She stilled, chewing that over. JD wouldn't be that sentimental…would he?

Her eyes unblinking, Candy slowly walked towards the far left wall of the office, coming to a halt before the aged photograph. They looked happy in the scene, she thought. Dressed in wedding clothing, grinning at each other as if they'd never seen a happier day, the bride and groom resembled two lovesick puppies as they lifted a piece of wedding cake to the other's mouth.

Candy blinked, remembering the key. And the fact that time was of the essence.

She shook off the reverie and slowly lifted her hands to the portrait. Twisting her robe-clad body so that she could easily glance behind it, she somehow wasn't surprised when she found a small key taped to the back of it. *So he is that sentimental…*

Quickly and carefully removing the key, she settled the portrait against the wall and scurried back over to the desk. *Come on, come on. He could wake up at any time.*

She sank the key into the socket. A perfect fit.

Breathing deeply, Candy opened the desk drawer, hoping to find some sort of paperwork that would explain what had become of her family. There were no phones on the island. Only the singular cell phone JD carried in his pocket like an appendage.

Her hand stilled as the drawer opened. Her forehead wrinkled. There was nothing inside of the drawer, she thought, perplexed. Nothing but a...

"Photo album?" she murmured.

Confused, and more than a little curious, Candy's hands reached for the expensive leather album and plucked it up from its previous confinement. The leather looked worn, as if her husband had spent many hours looking through the photographs inside.

Her heart wrenched as she wondered to herself just whose pictures would be inside. The redhead perhaps? Or some other beautiful, statuesque woman he'd had to give up in order to see his revenge against the Morgans through?

Her heart beating madly, Candy laid the leather-jacketed book down on the desk and thrust it open. Feeling sick at her stomach at the thought of who might be inside, she told herself she didn't care, but knew that she did. Her hand stilled as she came to the first photograph.

"It's me," she whispered, her amber eyes wide. She thumbed through the album, quickly scanning the contents of every page. "These pictures are all of me."

Stunned, and more confused than ever before, Candy went back to the beginning and took her time studying the photographs. There she was at eighteen, shyly smiling up to her prom date. At nineteen when she'd been promoted to a VP's assistant at Morgan Chemicals. At twenty when mother had thrown a ball in her name. At twenty-one when she'd graduated from Harvard. At twenty-two when she'd been promoted to the vice-president of marketing...

"My God," she breathed out. "What is going on?"

"I should have hid that better," JD muttered from across the room, inducing her breathing to still. She glanced up, noting that he had put on his trousers but nothing else before he'd come to find her.

"JD," she murmured, her eyes unblinking. "What is this?"

One eyebrow came up sardonically. "You don't recognize yourself?" He sighed as he absently scratched his chin and looked away. "It's you Candy," he said softly. "All of the photos are of you."

She could see that. But she was still too shocked to speak. No man had thought enough of her before to so much as keep her picture in his wallet, yet JD had built a leather-encased shrine to her.

Candy simply watched him, too stunned to speak, waiting for him to reveal more.

"Lawrence promised you to me," he murmured, standing up straight from his previous slouch against the wall. "For years, I was told that you and I would be married one day."

Her eyes widened.

JD shoved his hands in the pockets of his trousers. "But Lawrence set me up and fired me for things I never did. And then you were gone." He sighed, his blue gaze at last meeting hers. "I spent years believing you would be mine one day, Candy Marie. The job, the money — none of it meant a damn thing. But I couldn't accept losing you too. Not when I'd worked so hard all of those years to make you proud of me."

Goosebumps went down her spine. "Proud of you?" she whispered, her heartbeat quickening. "Why on earth would you think I wouldn't be proud of you as is?"

He shrugged, but she could tell the subject was a painful reminder of something. Perhaps his past. A past she knew almost nothing of.

"Because I was a nobody," he murmured. "I was a nobody in love with a somebody. Aspiring to marry you was like a coal miner aspiring to marry royalty."

She felt tears gathering in the backs of her eyes. "You loved me?" she quietly asked.

His intense gaze bore into hers. "Always," he whispered.

She blinked, her eyelashes batting away the tears that kept threatening to fall. She closed the album and ran a hand over the leather exterior, then carefully placed it back in the drawer. In a daze, she looked back up to her husband. "I don't know what to say." She took a deep breath. "It certainly puts a new perspective on things."

JD stared at her for what felt like forever before he spoke again. "Yes, it does."

She nibbled on her lower lip. There was something different about him now. As if he'd been hoping she'd say or do something that she hadn't done.

Like admit that she had always loved him too?

Candy wasn't given any time to sort out her dazed emotions. The next thing she knew, JD was walking into the office and rifling through his desk drawers.

"Here," he said, handing her a piece of paper. She glanced down, noting that it was the very paper she needed to hold onto Morgan Chemicals. "I now realize that you didn't have anything to do with it. I never should have tried to make you pay for your father's sins. He took you away from me. But it's taken me all of this time to realize that I never really had you."

Her eyes widened. In surprise, in alarm of what she feared he was about to say — she didn't know.

"Go back to Atlanta," he murmured.

"JD — "

"Please," he said softly, his eyes closing for a brief moment. He ran a weary hand over his stubbly jaw. "I thought I could settle for taking you by force, but I guess I'm not as ruthless as I hoped I was."

He walked away from her then, his face carefully stoic. He stopped at the doors before walking over the threshold, long enough to look back at her with those lost, haunted eyes of his. Now she understood why they were always so intense when she was near him. He had done all of this just so he could have *her*. It had never been about revenge. "I love you, Candy Marie. Now. Then. Always."

And then he was gone.

Candy's hand flew up to cover her mouth. Numb, she sank down into the leather chair behind the desk and stared at nothing for the better part of an hour. She felt like she was dreaming. She felt lost in the surreal haze that had engulfed her.

James Douglas Mahoney III loved *her?* He had always loved *her?* Ordinary, unglamorous Candace Marie Morgan?

She swallowed roughly. As if some invisible dam inside of her broke, she gasped and let the tears fall freely.

She had always loved him too. Now. Then. Always. Just as he'd said to her. She should have spoken up. She should have told him how she felt…

Snapping out of her previous stupor, Candy bolted up from the leather chair and raced from the office. It couldn't be too late, she told herself. It just couldn't be.

The robe she wore dangled open as she raced to find JD. Heedless of her exposed body, she flew up the stairs, not stopping until she reached their bedroom. By the time she thrust open the double doors, her breathing was labored and perspiration dotted her forehead.

He was gone, she thought, her heart wrenching as she looked around the room that had once been filled with her husband's personal items. He was already gone.

"Oh no," she whispered, sinking down onto the bed. "Oh JD."

Jaid Black

Chapter 8
Three days later

JD sighed as he glanced around the empty medieval looking estate he'd had built over a year ago. He was the only person of money and prestige in Atlanta who didn't own a home with either a Victorian design or one with an antebellum influence. He had gone for the Baroque look because Lawrence had once mentioned that it was Candy's favorite.

He poured himself a brandy and plopped down on a chair before the large, Old World style fireplace. He had been foolish to let her go, he decided. Perhaps he could have lived with taking her by force if it was the only way he could have her.

It certainly beat the hell out of being without her.

Lost in his thoughts, he absently glanced toward the oversized chair set on the far side of the library. He sipped from his brandy as he looked back to the fireplace — then did a double take.

Candy.

She was here. Naked, sitting on the oversized chair, her legs splayed wide, dangling from either arm.

JD quickly set down his brandy before he spilled it.

"That was pretty unsporting of you to go back on our agreement," Candy said as her right hand lazily stroked that delicious, bald cunt of hers. "Don't one of those eight thousand Clauses of yours cover what happens to the recalcitrant husband when he walks out on his wife?"

He sat there for a long moment, simply staring at her. "No," he at last murmured, rising up from his chair. His penis was so swollen it ached. "They don't."

Candy raised one blonde eyebrow. "Then I want you to sign a new agreement tomorrow. Because if you walk out on me again—"

"I never walked out. I thought you didn't want me."

"—Because if you walk out on me again then I reserve the right to...well, I don't know what right I want precisely. I'll have to figure that out." That gorgeous eyebrow of hers shot up again. "We can make that Clause eight zillion and nine."

JD held back a smile. "Why are you here?" he whispered.

She sighed as if she was the sole martyr for the entire female race and he was the idiot male representing the opposition. Much to his surprise, she pulled a photo-static copy of their marriage agreement out from behind her and held it up. He blinked.

"According to Clause 76, I, the undersigned, am supposed to offer my body as a sperm receptacle to my husband twice daily, every day, for as long as we both shall live."

JD winced at the callous wording of the document. He glanced away, clearing his throat.

"I haven't offered myself as a sperm receptacle in three days. That means I owe you six orgasms. I'm nothing like Lawrence. I always keep my part of a bargain, you see."

His intense gaze found hers. "Is that what this is?" he murmured. "Keeping your end of a deal?"

Her eyes gentled. "Of course not," she whispered, her demeanor growing serious. She rose up from the oversized chair and stood before him.

"Then what is it?"

She smiled softly. "I love you, JD," she murmured. "I've loved you since I was a little girl and I'll go on loving you for the rest of my life."

His eyes searched her face as if looking for the truth.

"If you would have given me time to recover from the greatest shock of my life before dashing off to Atlanta like the dramatic, ill-fated heroine of a gothic novel, I would have said those words three days ago."

He grinned. Their gazes clashed and locked.

"It's been the worst three days of my life," he admitted.

"Mine too." She smiled. "But let's put the past behind us. All of it," she said meaningfully. She cocked her head. "Okay?"

For an answer, he kissed her. One minute she was on her feet and the next minute she was swept up into his arms, her tongue seeking his, as he carried her over to the rug before the fireplace. He came down on his knees and set her before him, growling into her mouth as her hands feverishly plucked at his clothing.

"I want you so much," she whispered as she tore her lips away from his. Her voice sounded breathless, her lips looked well-kissed. "I used to lie in bed at night when I was a girl and fantasize about being in your arms, in your bed."

He both hated and loved what the confession did to his heart. Hated it because men weren't supposed to be affected by words like that to the point of grinning like an idiot, and yet he was. Loved it because it meant that this moment was real—and that Candace Marie Morgan was finally all his.

Without force.

JD nudged his wife down onto the ground, thrusting her legs apart as he came down on top of her. Desperate to be inside of her, he impaled his swollen cock inside of her, seating himself to the hilt. "You don't want to know," he panted, "how many of my masturbation fantasies you've starred in."

She grinned back, apparently loving that confession. He rotated his hips and slammed into her again, causing her expression to go serious as she hissed.

Candy thrust her breasts up. "I love it when you suck on my nipples while we have sex," she breathily admitted. "Could you do that again?"

Could he? It's damn near all he'd thought about these past three days and nights.

JD lowered his face down to her breasts with a growl, his tongue wrapping around one of her erect nipples. He vigorously sucked on it as he plunged into her flesh, his hips rocking back and forth as he buried his cock inside of her over and over, again and again.

Just as he'd always wanted it to be. Just as it now was.

The sins of Lawrence Morgan have come full circle...

As he made love to his wife, it occurred to JD that he had accomplished something far more meaningful than infiltrating Lawrence's precious company, something far more powerful than infiltrating the bastard's precious bloodline:

He had managed to find happiness with Lawrence's daughter. He had infiltrated Candy's heart and she his. Everything was finally as it should be.

JD smiled down to his wife as he made love to her, all thoughts of the past firmly relegated to the cobwebs of his memories.

Epilogue
Five years later

"He's so handsome," Candy breathed out, a paper plate filled with a huge piece of chocolate cake clutched to her chest. She bit her lip as she watched JD Mahoney spike the volleyball a final time, thereby winning the game for his team at the Morgan-Mahoney Chemical company picnic. "So handsome," she whispered.

Cheers rang up from the crowd as Candy dreamily studied JD's features. His muscular, athletic body. His chiseled face and gorgeous dark hair. His...

She smiled. They'd made love less than three hours ago. She shouldn't be thinking about that already.

"You did it!" a feminine voice chirped as a gorgeous, petite brunette threw herself into JD's arms. "You're my hero," she said excitedly, her tiny, perfect hands settling on his cheeks.

JD grinned. "Your hero, huh?" He tickled her until she squealed. "Give daddy a kiss, munchkin."

Candy closed her eyes, her heart soaring. She still couldn't believe how happy she was. After all of these years as his wife, she still got weak-kneed at the very sight of him. Life had turned out better than she'd ever dreamed possible.

"Candy, honey," JD called from across the field. "Where are you?"

She opened her eyes and smiled. "Right here," she piped up, waddling out of the shadows to meet up with him and their daughter. Her pregnant stomach was so huge she felt like she was about to pop.

His intense gaze possessively flicked over her swollen belly, then up to her breasts and face. "You ready to go home, babe?"

"Definitely."

JD's face scrunched up as he lassoed one muscular arm around her. "Something wrong, sweetheart?"

Candy smiled up to him. She shook her head, then laid it against his shoulder as the three of them walked towards the awaiting limo. "Not at all," she whispered. "Everything is very right."

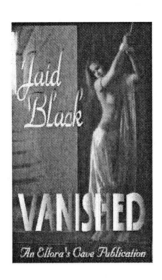

The following excerpt from the novella "Vanished", © Jaid
Black,   2002,   is   available   in   e-book   format   at
http://www.ellorascave.com.

Chapter 1

She'd give anything for some coffee. An oversized mug filled to the rim with the richest, hottest, blackest Columbian elixir ever to grace a coffee cup would have felt like a gift from the gods right about now. But at this point, she thought grimly, even a half-filled Dixie cup that tasted more like water than beans would be enough to make her do a cartwheel.

Lynne Temple sighed as her red SUV idled up yet another twisting, snowy mountain road. She'd been following this temporary route for over an hour now and was beginning to worry that someone had neglected to put up a very necessary sign that would have kept her from heading in the wrong direction.

A semi had jackknifed on the turnpike an hour or so before she'd gotten to it, making the lanes impassable. The police quickly threw up a temporary detour route through the rocky terrain, diverting traffic through a small coalminer town in the remote wilds of West Virginia. Not that there was much traffic in need of being diverted at eleven o'clock on a Tuesday night in a sparsely populated, rural area. Indeed, Lynne had yet to run into another pair of headlights.

For the first time since this little excursion off the beaten path began, a sense of alarm was beginning to settle in. It was pitch black outside, nothing but the SUV's high beams to break the bleak darkness. The further she drove through the steep terrain, the thicker the wintry forests on either side of the tiny road grew. It was creepy out here, she thought, the tiny hairs at the nape of her neck stirring. Dark, remote, and creepy.

She didn't belong in this place, she knew. Lynne felt — and was — out of her element. To a city girl from the flatlands of Clearwater, Florida, even something as simple as driving on the turnpike set her nerves on edge. The snowy mountains the turnpike cut through were steeper than she'd ever seen. The winds this high up in altitude were harsh during the winter months, beating against the SUV and making her feel as though she would be blown off the side of a cliff at any given moment. She felt no more protected from the elements than she would have felt driving a tin can with four glued-on wheels.

The turnpike had been bad enough. Driving through the bizarre little twisting road nestled somewhere up in the Appalachians was a thousand times worse.

Lynne took a deep breath and exhaled slowly, telling herself not to freak out. So it was dark outside. So the wind was moaning like a demon out of a B-movie. So the gravel road had turned to mud and slush about fifteen minutes ago…

"Great," she muttered under her breath. "This is just great."

She realized that she needed to turn around and follow the winding path back to some manner of civilization, but there wasn't precisely anywhere to turn around. She could stop in the middle of the "road", she supposed, and try to turn around that way, but with her luck she'd finally spot another vehicle while attempting the feat — as it slammed into the side of her new vehicle from out of nowhere.

At first she had assumed she was following the detour correctly, but she couldn't recall the last time she'd seen a sign. Worse yet, she'd made more than a few turns in the past hour and now wasn't altogether certain she could find her way back in the middle of the night. Especially when she considered that the snowfall had been light but steady, so the SUV's tracks were probably already covered up.

What an ironic way to start her new life, Lynne considered, frowning. Thirty-four was supposed to be the year she made life happen instead of waiting for it to come to her. She could design databases from anywhere, but since her largest client was located in the capitol city of Charleston, West Virginia, she'd decided to make the move after the divorce from Steve and settle into a lazy southern house down on the river that saw all four seasons. It sounded almost idyllic compared to the humid, forever hot beach apartment crammed full of bad memories she'd vacated all of a day ago. And it could still be idyllic—if only she could find her way back to the beaten path.

Lynne's gaze absently flicked toward the fuel tank gage. Her heart rate sped up when she saw that she was down to an eighth of a tank of gas. *Great!* she thought. *This is just damn great.* She blew out a breath, that sense of alarm growing by leaps and bounds. It was pitch black outside, the winds were moaning something fierce, she was driving up a muddy, slushy path that led only God knows where, the snowfall was picking up a bit, and now the SUV was running on fumes. She would have laughed if only she weren't so terrified.

Clutching the steering wheel so tightly her knuckles turned white, Lynne's dark brown eyes widened as the narrow path she was traveling up became impossibly narrower. "Shit," she mumbled, deciding it was way past time to turn around. The snow-capped forest to either side of the tiny road was growing thicker...and somehow a lot more intimidating.

Her teeth sank into her lower lip; perspiration broke out on her forehead. She absently tucked a rogue strand of dark brown hair behind an ear as her inner musings turned ugly. As ridiculous as it sounded even to herself, she was afraid to stop the SUV long enough to turn it around. Stopping equaled vulnerability, leaving her naked to outside attack, even if the stop would only last a few seconds.

Lynne blew out a breath, rolling her eyes at her dramatic thoughts. "You've watched one too many horror movies, kiddo," she whispered as she let up on the gas pedal and slowly worked the brake. She hadn't seen another vehicle let alone another person for miles — well over an hour ago by now. The chances of some psycho on the loose nabbing her while she did an about-face in a locked vehicle of all things was about nil to none.

The SUV came to a stop, the lack of movement underscoring the sound of the moaning Appalachian winter wind outside the barricade of the windows. She told herself to ignore it, to forget about the fact she was alone in the middle of a mountaintop forest in the dead of night, and to concentrate on getting the hell out of there.

Backing up enough to turn the vehicle around, she gasped when a movement of some sort snagged her peripheral vision. Her breathing immediately stilled. She blinked and did a double take.

"Damn, damn, damn," she murmured as she kept turning the SUV around. She prayed she was imagining things because she hadn't seen anyone or anything upon second glance. *Just get out of here!* she told herself as the vehicle straightened and she stepped on the accelerator. *Now!*

Flooring it, Lynne's heart rate went over the top as she slammed down on the gas pedal. Probably not the swiftest reflex she'd ever had, for the SUV immediately went into a skid. Mingled mud and ice-slush flew up from all sides, pelting the windshield and making her heart thump like a rock in her chest.

Another movement to the left…

Lynne barely had time to register that she'd seen something when the shadow of a large man appeared from seemingly out of nowhere. She screamed as she slammed down on the brakes and veered a quick right to avoid hitting him, then screamed again when she momentarily lost control of the SUV and it went into a flat spin.

Shaking like a leaf, she tried to recover from the spin, but it was too late. Her eyes widened as the vehicle skidded off the narrow path and headed straight for the trunk of a thick oak tree. Unable to do anything besides go numb from shock, she watched in helpless horror as her brand new cherry red vehicle collided with a mighty oak, smashing the entire front end and simultaneously jarring her body. Frantic, she turned her head to the left to see if that man was still around — or if she'd imagined him altogether.

The automatic airbag in the steering column engaged and a second later she was struck in the side of the head with a life-saving device that damn near killed her. She gasped as the airbag assaulted her, her dark eyes rolling back into her head.

Please don't let me pass out, she thought in terror as the shadow of a very real, and very large, man emerged from the forest. *Oh God — oh please — I must have sustained a concussion…*

Lynne's vision began to dim at the precise moment the stranger's form appeared in her remaining headlight and began to steadily walk toward her SUV. He was huge—at least a foot taller than her own five feet—and was wearing a one-piece jumper of some sort. His face was grim, his sharp gaze intense.

As her eyes slowly began to close, she considered the possibility that maybe the stranger was a mechanic. Mechanics tended to wear those blue issue one-piece jumpsuits. Maybe he could even help fix the SUV.

Her dulling gaze flicked toward the stranger's vein-roped hands. Hysteria bubbled up inside of her when she saw that his hands were chained together. And, she thought, ice-cold horror lancing through her, so were his ankles...

Lynne's heart violently pumped away in her chest even as she slipped into the black void of unconsciousness. He was an escaped convict, her mind screamed, the reality that she was about to pass out unavoidable. Oh God—

Oh please, she thought as her eyes irrevocably closed, *please somebody help me!*

SURRENDER

Written by

Lora Leigh

Dedicated to: My sister Lue Anne, who's always there, no matter what. Thanks, Sis. You make life easier when it gets really hard.

Chapter 1

"Tess, you coming to my party?" It was her father's voice on her answering machine that finally roused her from sleep. "You better be here, girl. I'm tired of you staying away. You call me back."

The line disconnected. Tess sighed as she opened her eyes. She would have preferred the dream to the stark loneliness that awaited her when she opened her eyes. At least there, even in the dark, frightening abyss of desires too dark to name, she had a purpose, rather than her fears.

She stared down at the large stuffed gorilla she clutched to her chest in her sleep. A present from her father when she left with her mother. Something to keep the bad dreams away, he had said sadly, even though she had been an adult. Tess often had bad dreams.

Perhaps she shouldn't have left as well, Tess often thought. She was just entering college at the time, and could have made her own choice. But her mother had needed her. Or Tess had thought she did. Now she wasn't certain if her mother needed her, or merely needed to control her.

"Tess, you awake now?" Her mother, Ella James called from the bottom of the downstairs hallway, her voice barely penetrating the distance.

Tess had installed her own phone line straight out of college and moved her bedroom to the upper floor where her mother rarely ventured. She needed her privacy, and her mother was prone to butt in wherever she could. The stairs kept her from venturing into Tess's privacy very often.

"Yeah, Mom. I'm awake," she yelled back, rising from bed, imagining her mother's moue of distaste. It was Saturday, for God's sake. She was entitled to sleep in. She could just imagine her mother's expression if she knew it was her father's call that woke her.

Resigned, Tess got of bed and headed for the shower.

Tess was well aware of her mother's disgust for her father's lifestyle. Jason Delacourte didn't stay home or keep regular hours or play the nine to five game. He owned a national electronics corporation and lived the lifestyle he chose. He gave dinners, attended charities and threw yearly parties. Ella preferred her books and her quiet and anything that didn't involve a man. She had done her best to raise her daughter the same way.

Tess did hate parties. She always had and she knew she always would. She invariably ended up going alone. Always ended up leaving alone. Parties jinxed her. Men jinxed her, they had for years. But she was committed to this party. She had promised. What could she do but get ready to go?

She grimaced, confused as she pondered her lack of a love life. Or perhaps sex life. She wasn't a great believer in love or the happily ever after stuff. She had rarely seen it work, her own parents were an example of that one. And her father's second marriage seemed more rocky than solid.

She frowned as she usually did when she thought of her father's new wife. Well, perhaps not new. Jason Delacourte, her father, had been married for nearly three years now to Melissa. The woman still insisted that everyone call her Missy. As though she were still a teenager. Tess snarled with distaste. Of course, the woman was barely thirty-five, ten years younger than her father, and nearly ten years older then Tess. The least he could have done, she sniped silently, was marry a woman closer to his own age.

She could barely tolerate being in the same room with 'Missy'. The woman gave dumb blonde a new meaning. How she managed to be related to a man touted as a genius, Tess had no idea. But she was. Cole Andrews was Missy's brother, and Tess's father swore Cole had moved Delacourte Electronics into the financial sphere it now enjoyed as one of the leading electronic manufacturers. The thought of him caused mixed reactions in Tess, though.

Cole was six feet three inches of hard packed muscle and dark, brooding good looks with a cynical, mocking attitude that drove her crazy. His kisses were the stuff dreams were made of. His fingers were wicked instruments of torturous pleasure; his lips were capable of throwing her into a hypnotic trance when they touched her.

She suppressed a sigh. No man kissed as good as Cole Andrews. It should be a crime that one man should ooze so much sex appeal, and be such an asshole to boot. And it was really a crime that she couldn't get past that one stolen kiss long enough to enjoy any others.

After showering, she quickly blow dried her hair, sighing as she swiped the brush through her shoulder-length black hair one last time before turning back to the open doors of her large closet. She had enough clothes. One thing her father had always done was made certain she was well provided for.

Elementary school teachers didn't make a lot in terms of money, and it wasn't the glamorous job Jason Delacourte had always thought his daughter should hold, but it was what she wanted to do. Besides, it kept her out of the social sphere her stepmother and Cole Andrews moved in. That was a big enough plus to keep her there.

But, she had promised her father she would stay with him for this one week. That she would take the time off work and return to the large family home she had grown up in before his divorce from her mother, and she would try to be his daughter.

It wasn't that she didn't love him, she thought as she packed her suitcase. She did. She loved her father terribly, but Cole was at the house. He stayed there often, and it was Cole she needed to avoid.

After packing the more casual clothes she would need and her treasured, hidden vibrator, Tess moved back to her closet to choose what she would wear for the yearly Valentine's Day party her father gave. It was also the third year anniversary of his marriage to Missy. Yeah, she really wanted to celebrate that one.

She pulled a short, black, silk sheath from the closet and hung it on the doorknob. From her dresser she pulled out a black thong, a lacy matching bra, and smoky silk stockings. The dark colors suited her mood. Valentine's Day was for lovers, and Tess didn't have one. She still didn't understand why she was going to this stupid party.

It wasn't like her father would really miss her. The house would be packed. They didn't need her there. She hadn't attended one of Missy's parties in well over a year now. They were loud, bustling and often turned out a bit too wild for her tastes. Besides, Cole always ended up bringing his latest flame, and pissing her off the first hour into it.

His dark blue eyes would watch her, faintly cynical, always glittering with interest while the bimbos at his side simpered adoringly. She snorted. If she had to simper to hold him, well then—

She sighed desolately. She would probably simper if she thought it would help. If she could learn how. Her mouth always seemed to get the better of her though. His general air of superiority just grated on her. Ever since that first kiss, his hard body holding her captive against the wall as he whispered what he wanted in her ear. Her body had sung in agreement, her mind, shocked and dazed from the images, had kicked in with an instant defense: her smart mouth.

It had been over two years.

She sat down on the bed, still naked, her cunt wet, throbbing at the memory.

"Can you take the heat, baby?" he had whispered to her, holding her against the wall as he ground his cock between her thighs. "I won't lie to you, Tess. I want you bad. But I'm not one of your little college boys that you can mess with. I want you tied to my bed, screaming, begging for me. I want to pump my dick in that tight little ass of yours, I want to hear your cries while I'm buried there and fuck you with a dildo bought just for that tight cunt of yours."

She shook now in remembered arousal and hot desperate need.

"Sure," she had bit out. "And then I can fuck your ass next!"

He had had the nerve to laugh at her. Laugh at her as his fingers sank into the wet, tight grip of her pussy and her orgasm rippled over her body. She'd gasped, feeling the slick heat as it pulsed through her vagina, washing over his fingers. Then he had slid them down to the tight little hole he had promised to fuck, one finger sinking in to its first knuckle, sending a flare of pain through her body that she had enjoyed too much to be comfortable with.

Tess remembered her fear, throbbing as hot as her lust. She had pushed him away, trembling, unfamiliar with the hot pulse of hunger that had flared in her, unlike anything she had known before. And he had watched her, his cock a thick, hard outline beneath his pants, his eyes dark as she stood before him trembling.

"Pervert!" she had accused him.

His lips had quirked, his eyes flaring in anger.

"And you?" he asked her. "What does that make you, baby? Because sooner or later, you'll have to admit you want it."

"What, raped?" she had bit out.

His eyes suddenly softened, a strange smile quirking his lips.

"Never rape, Tess. You'll beg me for it. Because we both know you want it as much as I do. My cock sliding up your tight ass while you scream for me to stop, then screaming for me to never stop. You're mine Tess, and I know what it takes to give you what you need. When you're ready to accept that, let me know."

Tess shook her head. Wanting it and accepting it were two different things. She had dreamed of it ever since, too humiliated to ask him for it, and he refused to offer a second time.

She touched her smooth, waxed pussy, her eyes closing as she lay back on the bed. The thought of what he wanted terrified her, yet it aroused her to the point of pain. The thought of his cock, so thick and hard, easing into her ass as he penetrated her wet, pleading cunt with a dildo, her tied down, unable to fight, unable to escape whatever he desired, had her soaked with need. He wouldn't hurt her. She knew enough about Cole to know he would never hurt her, but he could show her things she wasn't sure she was ready to know about herself. He could show her a part of herself that she wasn't certain she could handle. That was a frightening thought.

Her fingers eased through the shallow, narrow crease of her cunt, circled her clit. He had promised to eat her there. To run his tongue around her clit, suck it, eat her like honey, a lick at a time. She shuddered, moaning, imagining her finger was his tongue, licking at her cunt, lapping at the slick heat that soaked her pussy. She circled her clit, whispering his name, then moved her fingers back down to the desperate ache in her vagina. She penetrated the tight channel with two of her fingers, biting her lip, wondering how thick and long Cole's fingers would be inside her. He had such a big hands, he would fill her, make her scream for more.

He had whispered the dark promise that he would fuck her ass, take her there, make her scream for him. She bit her lips, her fingers moving, one inserting into that tiny, dark hole while she wished she hadn't packed her vibrator so quickly. As her finger passed the tight entrance, she allowed two fingers of her other hand to sink into her vagina. She could hear his voice in the back of her mind, feel his finger, thicker than hers, spearing a dart of pleasurable pain through her as he pierced her ass. And he had told her, warned her he would fuck her there.

Her knees bent, her hips thrusting harder against her own fingers as she imagined Cole between her thighs, licking her, fucking her with his fingers, driving her over the edge as they fucked into her; her cunt, her ass, until—

She cried out as the soft ripples of release washed over her. Her vagina clenched on her fingers, her womb trembling with pleasure. It wasn't the release she had experienced with Cole's fingers or her vibrator, but it took the edge off the lust that seemed to only grow over time.

Chapter 2

It wasn't enough. An hour and a cold shower later, Tess's body still simmered with need. Stretched on her bed, her body sheened with sweat as she fought for orgasm, she cursed the phone when it rang at her side. Grimacing when it refused to stop, Tess reached over, grabbing the receiver.

"Hello." She tried to clear her throat, to still her rapid breaths, and hoped she could explain it away if it was her father. She didn't want him to know his daughter was a raging mass of horny hormones ready to explode.

There was a brief silence, as though the caller were weighing his words.

"Feeling better?" A trace of knowing mockery, a deep, sensually husky voice whispered the words.

Tess flushed at Cole's voice. Damn him.

"I haven't been sick," she bit out, her eyes closing as her vagina pulsed. She smoothed her fingers over her clit, feeling the increased stimulation there. Damn, she could get off with just his voice.

"No, just trying to get off," he said lazily. "I would help. All you have to do is ask."

Ask, ask, her inner voice begged.

"In your dreams." She winced as the words burst from her mouth. Damn him, he put her on the defensive faster than anyone she knew.

"It would appear in yours as well," he said, his mockery suddenly gone. "I know how you sound when you're aroused, Tess. Don't try to lie to me. Let me hear you. Touch yourself for me."

Tess felt her breath strangle in her throat.

"You're a pervert, Cole." She fought for her own control at the sound of that sexy voice. "Isn't phone sex illegal?"

"I'm sure most of what I want to do with you could be termed illegal," he chuckled. "Let's talk about it, Tess. Come on, tell me what you were doing to yourself. Are you using your fingers or a vibrator?"

"I do not have a vibrator." She clenched her teeth over the lie.

"Dildo?" he whispered the words heatedly. "Are you fucking yourself, Tess? Thinking about me, how much I want you?"

"No!" She clenched the receiver in her hand, shaking her head despite the fact that her fingers had returned to her suddenly pulsing cunt.

"I'd like to see you in my bed, Tess, your legs spread, your hands touching your pretty cunt, fucking yourself. Did I ever tell you I bought that dildo I promised you? It's nice and thick, Tess. Almost as large as my cock. I want to watch you use it. See you fuck yourself with it."

"God, Cole," she gasped. "We're on the phone. This is indecent." But her fingers were sinking into her cunt.

"What were you doing before I called, Tess?" His voice was dark, hot. "I know you were touching yourself. I know the sound of your voice when you're ready to come, and you're ready to come, baby."

"No—" She tried to deny the obvious truth, but she couldn't keep her breath from catching as her fingers grazed her clit once again.

"Son of a bitch, Tess," he growled. "Are you close, baby?" His voice deepened. "If I were there, I'd make you scream for it. I'd fuck you so deep and hard you wouldn't be able to stop it. You'd cum for me, Tess. Come for me now, baby. Let me hear you."

His voice was so deep, so sensual and aroused it caused her womb to contract almost painfully. Her body bowed, her breath catching on a near sob. He brought all her darkest desires, her deepest fantasies to the forefront of her mind. It terrified her.

"Cole," she whispered his name, wanting to deny him, but her fingers weren't listening as they stroked her clit, sank into her vagina, then moved back to repeat the action.

She was so hot she could barely stand it. So horny she was on the verge of screaming for relief.

"I'm stroking my cock, Tess, listening to you lay there, imagining you touching your juicy cunt, wishing I were with you, watching you fuck yourself with the dildo I bought you." His words caused her to gasp, her womb to contract painfully, her hips to surge into her plunging fingers.

"No." She tossed her head. She couldn't do this.

"Damn, Tess, I want to fuck you," he growled, his voice rough. "I want to be buried so deep and hard inside you you'll never forget it or deny me again. Come for me, damn you. At least let me hear what I can't have. Fuck yourself Tess, give this to me. Those aren't your fingers buried in your pussy, it's my cock. Mine, and I'm going to fuck you until you scream."

Tess's orgasm ripped through her. She shuddered, whimpered, her body tightening to the point of pain before she felt her vagina explode.

"Oh God, Cole," she cried his name, then heard his hard exclamation of pleasure, knew he was coming, knew her climax had triggered his own as well.

"Tess," he groaned. "Damn you, when I get hold of you I'll fuck you until you can't walk."

Tess trembled at the erotic promise in his voice, the dark sensuality that terrified her, made her want to give him whatever he wanted.

"No," she whispered, fighting for breath, fighting for sanity. "I asked you to stay away."

She wanted to whimper, she wanted to beg.

There was silence over the line.

"Stay away?" he asked her carefully. "I don't think so, baby. I've stayed away too long as it is. You're mine Tess, and I'm going to prove it to you. All mine. In every way mine, and I'll be damned if I'll let you deny it any longer."

Chapter 3

Her mother was waiting on her when she came down the stairs, her suitcase in hand. Ella Delacourte was a small, spare woman, with dark brown hair and sharp hazel eyes. There were few things she missed, and even less that she was tolerant of.

"So you're still going," she snapped out as she eyed the suitcase Tess set by the front door. "I thought you would have more pride than that, Tess."

Tess pressed her lips together as she fought to keep her sarcastic reply in check.

"This has nothing to do with pride, Mother," she told her quietly. "He's still my father."

"The same father who destroyed your family. Who ensured you lost the home you were raised in," Ella reminded her bitterly. "The same father that married the whore who meant more to him than you did."

Tess's chest clenched with pain, and with anger. She wasn't a child anymore, and there were times when she could clearly see why her father had been unable to get along with her mother. Ella saw only one view, and that was hers.

"He took care of us, Mother," she pointed out. "Even after the divorce."

"As though he had a choice." Ella crossed her arms over her breasts as she stared at Tess in anger.

"Yes, Mother, he had a choice after I reached eighteen," Tess reminded her bleakly. "But I believe he still sends you money and provides whatever you need, just as he does me. He doesn't have to do this."

"Conscience money," Ella spat out, her pretty face twisting into lines of anger and bitter fury. "He knows he did us wrong, Tess. He threw us out—"

"No, you elected to leave, if I remember correctly." Tess wanted to scream in frustration.

The argument never ended. It was never over. She felt as though she continually paid for her father's choices because her mother had no way of making him pay.

"He's depraved. As though you need to spend a week in his house." Ella was shaking now with fury, contempt lacing each word out of her mouth. "Those parties he throws are excuses for orgies, and that wife of his—"

"I don't want to hear it, Mother—"

"You think your father and his new family are so respectable and kind," she sneered. "You think I don't know how you watched that brother of hers. That I didn't know about the flowers he sent you last year. They're monsters, Tess." She pointed a thin, accusing finger at Tess. "Depraved and conscienceless. He'll turn you into a tramp."

Tess felt her face flame. She had fought for years to hide her attraction to Cole. She had heard all the rumors, knew his sexual exploits were often gossiped about. He had more or less admitted them to her on several occasions.

"No one can turn me into a tramp, Mother," she bit out. "Just as there's no way you can change the fact that I have a father. I can't ignore him or pretend he doesn't exist, and I don't want to."

Tess faced her parent, feeling the same, horrible fear that always filled her at the thought of making her too angry. Of disappointing her in any way. But as she faced her fear, she felt her own anger festering inside her. For so many years she had tried to make up for the divorce her father had somehow forced. She knew he took the blame for it. Just as her mother vowed complete innocence. She was beginning to wonder if either of them would ever tell her the truth.

"You'll end up just like him," Ella accused, her eyes narrowing hatefully.

Tess could only shake her head.

"I'll be home in a week, Mother," she said, picking up her luggage.

In the back of her mind, she knew she would not be returning though. She had stayed out of guilt and out of fear of failing somehow in her mother's eyes. She was only now realizing, she could never succeed in her mother's opinion though. She was fighting a losing battle. A battle she didn't want to win to begin with.

* * * * *

Tess was still trembling when she pulled into the large circular driveway of her father's home. The shadows of evening were washing over his stately Virginia mansion, spilling long shadows over the three-story house and the tree shrouded yard. The drive from New York wasn't a hard one, but her nervousness left her feeling exhausted. She definitely wasn't up to facing Cole. Her face flushed at the thought. She had tried not to think about the phone call that morning, or the core of heat it had left lingering inside her.

It had nearly been enough to have her turning around several times and heading back to her safe, comfortable life in her mother's home. She would have too, until she thought of her mother. Ella was too frightened of the world to draw her head out of her books and see the things she was missing. She had lost her husband years before their divorce because of her distaste of his sexual demands. She told Tess often how disgusting, how shameful she found sex to be.

Tess didn't want to grow old, knowing she had passed up the exciting things in life. She didn't want to ache all her life for the one thing she needed the most and passed up. But she didn't want her heart broken. And Tess had a feeling Cole could break her heart.

She wanted him too badly. She had realized that in the past months. The dreams were driving her crazy. Dreams of Cole tying her to his bed, teasing her, touching her, his dark voice whispering his sexual promises to her. She was awaking more and more often, her cunt soaked, her breathing ragged, a plea on her lips.

Tess had known he was bad news even before her father married his sister. His eyes were too wicked, his looks too sensual. He was wickedly sexy, sinfully sensuous. She moaned in rising excitement and fear.

Leaving her keys in the ignition for the butler to park it, Tess jumped from the car. Night was already rolling in, and she would be damned if she would sit out in that car because she was too scared to walk into the house. Hopefully, Cole wouldn't be there. He wasn't always there.

"Good evening, Miss Delacourte." The butler, a large, burly ex-bouncer opened the door for her as she stepped up to it.

Thomas was well over fifty, Tess knew, but he didn't look a day over thirty-five. He was six feet tall, heavily muscled and sported a crooked nose and several small scars on his broad face. He was Irish, he said, with a mix of Cherokee Indian and German ancestry. His thick, brown hair was in a crew cut, his large face creased with a smile.

"Good evening, Thomas. Is Father in?" She stepped into the house, more uncomfortable than she had thought she would be.

This was the home she had grown up in, the one she had raced through with the puppy her father had once bought her, but her mother had gotten rid of. The home where her father had once patched skinned knees and a bruised heart. The home her mother had taken her out of when her father demanded his rights as a husband, or a divorce.

"Your father and Mrs. Delacourte are out for the evening, Miss," he told her as she stepped into the house. "Will you be staying for a while?"

"Yes." She took a deep breath. "My luggage is outside. Is my room still available?"

There was an edge of pain as she asked the question. She had learned that Missy had opened her room for guests, rather than keeping it up for Tess's infrequent returns.

"I'm sorry, Miss Tess," Thomas said softly. "The room is being redecorated. But the turret room is available. I prepared it myself this morning."

The turret room was the furthest away from the guest or family bedrooms. At the back of the house, on the third floor. The turret had been added decades ago by her grandfather and she had loved it as a child. Now she resented the fact that it was not a family room, but the one she knew Missy used for those visitors she could barely tolerate. Evidently, Tess thought, she had slipped a few notches in her stepmother's graces.

Tess breathed in deeply. Those weren't tears clogging her throat, she assured herself. Her chest was tight from exhaustion, not pain.

"Fine." She swallowed tightly. "Could you have my luggage brought up? I need a shower and some sleep. I'll see Father in the morning."

"Of course, Miss Tess." Thomas' voice was gentle. He had been with the family for as long as she could remember and she knew she wasn't hiding her pain from him.

"Is Father happy, Thomas?" she asked him as she paused before going down the hall to the hidden staircase that led to the turret room. "Does Missy take care of him?"

"Your father seems very happy to me, Miss Tess," Thomas assured her. "Happier than I've seen since Mrs. Ella left."

Tess nodded abruptly. That was all that mattered. She moved quickly down the hall, turning toward the kitchen then entering the staircase to the right. The staircase led to one place. The turret room.

It was a beautiful room. Rounded and spacious, the furniture had been made to fit the room exactly. The bed was large with a heavy, rounded walnut headboard that sat perfectly against the wall. Heavy matching drawers slid into the stone wall for a dresser, with a mantle above it to the side of the bed. Across the room was a small fireplace, the wood was gas logs, but it was pretty enough.

She felt like Cinderella before the Prince rescued her. Tess sat down heavily on the quilt that covered the bed. This sucked. She should get back in her car and head straight back home where she belonged. She didn't belong here anymore, and she was beginning to wonder if she ever had.

Taking a deep breath, she ran her hands through her hair and listened to Thomas coming up the stairs. He stepped into the room with a friendly smile, but his brown eyes were somber as they met hers.

"Will you be okay here, Miss Tess?" he asked her as he set the large suitcase and matching overnight bag on the luggage rack beside the door. "I could quickly freshen another room."

"No. I'm fine, Thomas." She shook her head. What was the point? She had come back, mainly to find something that didn't exist. It was best she learn that now, before it went any further.

Thomas nodded before going to the fireplace. With practiced moves he lit the gas fire, then pulled back and nodded in satisfaction at the even heat coming off the ceramic logs.

"Would you like me to announce dinner for you, Miss Tess?" he asked.

Her father and stepmother were away. Tess knew the servants would only be preparing their own food. She shook her head. They were all most likely anticipating a night to relax, she wouldn't deprive them of that. What hurt the most was her father's absence. He had known she was coming, and he wasn't here. It was the first time he had ever left, knowing she was coming home. The first time Tess had ever felt as though she were a stranger in her own home.

* * * * *

One thing Tess really liked about the turret room was the bathroom. The huge room was situated to the right of the bed, and held a large sunken tub big enough for three and a fully mirrored wall. Thomas had stocked the small refrigerator unit against her objections. One of his little surprises was a bottle of her favorite white wine. Tess opened it, poured a full glass and sipped at it as the water ran into the large ceramic tub. Steam rose around the room, creating an ethereal effect with the glow of the candles she had lit.

She stripped out of her jeans and T-shirt and setting the wineglass and bottle on a small shelf, sank into the bubbled liquid. Exquisite. She leaned back against the hand fashioned back of the tub and rested her head on the pillowed headrest. It was hedonistic. A wicked, sinful extravagance, as her mother would have said.

She closed her eyes and took a deep breath. She had expected her father to be home, had expected some sort of greeting. She didn't expect to be left on her own. But the sinful richness of the bathtub eased a bit of the hurt. She could enjoy this. This one last time.

She hadn't come home without ulterior motives, she knew. Perhaps this was her payment for it. It wasn't her father that had drawn her so much as the man that she knew would arrive sooner or later.

Cole. She took a deep breath, flushing once again at the memory of the phone conversation. She could handle a little sex with him. It wasn't like she was a virgin. It was the rest of it. Cole didn't go for just sex. Cole was wild and kinky and liked to spice things up, she had heard. Heard. She whimpered, remembering his promise to tie her to his bed and what he would do there.

She had never had rough sex, though she admitted, she had never had satisfying sex either. It had never been intense enough, strong enough. The hardest climax of her life had been in that damned hallway, with Cole's fingers thrusting inside her cunt. She had been so slick, so wet, that even her thighs had been coated with it.

Lifting the wineglass from the shelf, Tess sipped at it a bit greedily. Her skin was sensitive, her breasts swollen with arousal, her cunt clenching in need. Dammit, she should have found a nice, tame principal or teacher to satisfy her lusts with. Cole was bad news. She knew he was bad news. Had always known it.

She had known Cole before her father had married his sister. She had heard about his sexual practices, his pleasures. He was hedonistic, wicked. And sometimes, he liked to dominate. He wasn't a bully outside the bedroom. Confident, superior, but not a bully. But she had heard rumors. Tales of Cole's preferences, his insistence on submission from his women. The comments he had made to her over the years only backed up the rumors she had heard.

Tess trembled at the thought of being dominated by Cole. Equal parts fear and excitement thrummed through her veins, her cunt, swelling her breasts, making her nipples hard. She didn't need this. Didn't need the desire for him that she was feeling. Didn't need the broken heart she knew he could deal her. She drained the wine from her glass then poured another, realizing the effects of the drink were already beginning to travel through her system. She felt more relaxed, finally. She hadn't been this relaxed in months. Enjoying the sensations, she poured another, hoping she would at least manage a few hours of sleep tonight without dreaming of Cole.

Chapter 4

Tess came downstairs the next morning expecting to be greeted by her father. She had dressed in the dove gray sweater dress he had sent her the month before. Tiny pearl buttons closed it from the hem to just above her breasts. On her feet she wore matching pumps and pearls at her neck. Confident and sure of herself, Tess felt able to field her father's questions, his urgings that she move back home for a while. When she walked into the dimly lit family room, it was Cole she found instead.

She stood still, silent as she faced him across the room. His eyes, a brilliant blue and filled with wicked secrets, watched her narrowly. Thick, black lashes framed the brilliant orbs, just as his thick, black hair framed the savage features of his face. His cheekbones were high, sharp, his nose an arrogant slash down his face. His lips were wide, and could be full and sensual or thin with anger. Now, he seemed merely curious.

His arms were crossed over his wide, muscular chest, his ankles crossed as he stood propped against the back of a sectional couch that faced away from her.

"Where's Father?" Tess asked him, fighting her excitement, her own unruly desires.

"He was held up. He expects, perhaps, to be home tomorrow," he told her quietly.

"Perhaps?" She barely stilled the tremble in her voice.

"Perhaps." He straightened from his lazy stance, watching her with a narrow-eyed intensity that had her breasts and her cunt throbbing. Damn him for the effect he had on her.

"So he couldn't tell me himself?" she questioned him nervously, watching him advance on her, determined to stand her ground.

"I'm sure he'll call, eventually." His voice was a slow, lazy drawl, thick with tension and arousal. It was all she could do to keep her eyes on his face, rather than allowing them to lower to see how thick the bulge in his pants had grown. She knew for certain the throb in her vagina had intensified.

"So you volunteered as the welcome wagon?" She was breathless, and knew he could hear it in her voice. His eyes darkened with the knowledge, causing her heartbeat to intensify.

He moved steadily nearer, until he was only inches from her. She could feel the warmth of his body, and it tingled over her nerve endings. He was tall, so much broader than she. She felt at once threatened and secure. The alternating emotions had her caught, unable to move, unwilling to run.

The blood raced through her veins as she attempted to make sense of the powerful feelings racing through her body and her mind. Two years she had thought about him, fought the temptation he represented and the heat he inspired.

"I'm always here to welcome you, Tess." He smiled, that slow quirk of his lips that made the muscles in her stomach tighten. "But I have to admit, I was more than eager after talking to you yesterday."

Her face flamed. Echoes of her whimpers, her fight to breathe through her climax whispered through her mind. Cole's voice, husky and deep, urging her on, rough from his own arousal, then his own climax.

Tess swallowed hard as she caught her lip between her teeth in nervous indecision. Did she reach out for him? Should she run from him?

"Hound dog," she muttered, more angry at herself than she was at him.

He chuckled, his hand reaching out to touch the bare flesh at her neck.

"Prickly as ever I see," he said with a vein of amusement as his eyes darkened. "Would you be as hot in bed, Tess?"

"Like I would tell you!" she bit out.

She fought the instinct to lean closer to him, to inhale the spicy scent of aroused, determined male.

"Hmm, maybe you would show me," he suggested, his voice silky smooth, heated.

Tess trembled at the low, seductive quality of his voice. It traveled through her body, tightening her cunt, making her breasts swell, the nipples bead in anticipation. Her entire body felt flushed, hot. Then the breath became trapped in her throat. His hand moved, the backs of his fingers caressing a trail of fire to the upper mounds of her heaving breasts.

He looked into her eyes, his own slumberous now, heavy lidded.

"Mine," he whispered.

Her eyes widened at the possessive note in his voice.

"I don't think so." She wanted to wince at the raspy, rough quality of her voice. "I belong to no man, Cole. Least of all you."

So why was her body screaming out in denial? She could feel the bare lips of her cunt moistening as her body prepared itself for his possession. Her skin tingled, her mouth watered at the thought of his kiss.

"All mine," he growled as a single button slid free of its fragile mooring over her heaving breasts. "You knew there was no way I would stay away after hearing you climax to the sound of my voice, Tess. You knew I wouldn't let you go."

She shrugged, fighting for her composure, an independence that seemed more ingrained than needed at the moment.

"You don't have a choice but to let me go," she informed him, feeling trepidation dart through her at the sudden intensity in his eyes.

His fingers stroked over the rounded curve of her breast, his expression thoughtful as he stared down at her.

"Why are you fighting me, Tess?" he suddenly asked her softly. "For two years I've done everything but tie you down and make you admit to wanting me. And I know you do. So why are you fighting it?"

"Maybe I want to be tied down and forced to admit it," she said flippantly, ignoring the flare of excitement in her vagina at the thought. She had heard the rumors, knew the accusations her mother had heaped on her father's brother-in-law for years. "Yeah, Cole, me tied down, just waiting for you and one of your best buds. Hey hon, the possibilities are limitless here."

Her mouth was the bane of her existence. She mentally rolled her eyes at the sharp, mocking declaration.

"My best bud, huh?" He tilted his head, watching her with a slight smile.

"The more the merrier." She moved away from him, denying herself the touch she wanted above all others. "You know how it is. A girl has to have some kind of excitement in her life. May as well go all the way."

She was going to cut her own tongue out. Tess felt more possessed than in possession of any common sense at the moment. Tempting Cole, pushing him, was never a good idea. She knew that from experience. Yet it seemed she knew how to do little else.

"Tess, be careful what you wish for." He was openly laughing at her. "Have you ever had two men at once, baby?"

The endearment, softly spoken in that dark, wicked voice sent her pulse racing harder than before.

"Does it matter?" She turned back to him, some demonic imp urging her to tease, to tempt in return.

She flashed him a look from beneath her lashes, touching at his hips, suppressing her groan at the size of the erection beneath his jeans. Damn, he was going to bust the zipper any minute now.

"Doesn't matter." He crossed his arms over his chest. "I can give you whatever you want, Sugar. If you really want it. I'm flexible."

* * * * *

Cole felt his dick throb. Damn her, he knew she had no idea how far she truly was pushing him. He could see the excitement in her eyes, a glimmer of sexual heat, of determination. Did she think she could turn him off by giving him carte blanche to do his worse? She had no idea how sexual he could get. The thought of tying her down, forcing her to admit the needs of her body, or his needs, was nearly more than his self-control could bear. The thought of introducing her to the pleasures of a *ménage a trois*, hearing her screams of pleasure echo in his ears, had his cock so hard it was a physical ache.

He wanted Tess to have every touch, every sexual experience she could ever imagine wanting to try. He wanted her hot, wet, and begging for his cock. He wanted her to admit to her needs, just as he finally admitted to his own. He wanted Tess, now, tomorrow, forever. However he could get her, every way she would let him have her.

Cole watched the flush that mounted her cheekbones, the flare of interest in her eyes that she quickly doused. She thought it a game, a sexual repartee that she could easily brush aside later. But it didn't change the fact that Tess had given such ideas more than a passing thought. He could see it in the hard rise and fall of her breasts, the swollen curve of them, the hard points of her nipples. They were nearly as hard as his cock.

She couldn't know, he thought with a thread of amusement, just how much he would enjoy doing both things with her. The dominance level he possessed was incredibly high. Introducing her to being tied down, teased, tormented, or sandwiching her between his body and Jesse's—

He had to forcibly tamp down his lust. Not that sharing her would be easy, or would happen often, but there was a particular pleasure in it that could be found in no other sexual act. The thought of total control of her body, her desires and her lusts was an aphrodisiac nearly impossible to resist.

"Tess, you shouldn't dare me," he warned her carefully. "You don't know what you could be asking for, baby."

He felt honor bound to give her one chance, and one chance only, to still the raging desires building inside him. She didn't know, couldn't know the sexuality that was so much a part of him. A sexuality and dark desire he had been willing to dampen for her. But her bold declaration that she could handle them was more than he could resist.

"Maybe I do know." He loved the breathless quality in her voice, the edge of fear and lust in her voice was a heady combination.

"I would fuck your ass, Tess," he growled advancing on her once again. "Is that what you want? My best bud sinking in that tight pussy while I push inside your back hole. You would scream, baby."

The idea of it was making him so hot he could barely stand the heat himself.

"Hmm…" Her pink lips pouted into a moue of thoughtfulness. "Sounds interesting, Cole. But you know, I couldn't allow just anyone such privileges." She sighed regretfully. "Sorry, darling, but it appears you're out of luck."

Oh, she was in trouble. Cole kept his expression only slightly amused, allowing his sweet Tess to dig her own grave.

"And what qualities must a man have to be so lucky?" he asked her as he deliberately maneuvered her against the wall, his body pressing against hers, not forcing her, but holding her, warming her.

For a moment, an endearing vulnerability flashed in her eyes. His heart softened at what he read there. Mingled hope and need, a flash of uncertainty.

"Something you don't have." He wondered if she heard the regret in her voice.

"And what would that be, baby?" He wanted to pull her to his chest, hold her, assure her that anything she needed, anything she wanted, was hers for the asking.

She pushed away from him, her natural defensiveness taking over again, that flash of pain in her eyes overriding her need to play, to tease and tempt.

"Heart, Cole. It takes a heart," she bit out. "And I really don't think you have one."

* * * * *

Tess walked away quickly, anger enveloping her. It did little to tamp the desire or the raging cauldron of emotions that threatened to swamp her. Damn. Double damn. She couldn't love him. She couldn't need his love. Two years of sparring with him, fighting his advances and his heated looks couldn't have caused this.

She felt her body trembling, her chest tightening with tears. Loving Cole was hopeless. She didn't stand a chance against the sophisticated, experienced women he often slept with. She had seen them, hated them. Knowing he took them to his bed, made them scream for his touch was more than she could bear. Surely she didn't love him. But Tess had a very bad feeling she did.

Chapter 5

Tess came awake hours later, a sense of being watched, studied, breaking through the erotic dream of Cole teasing her, tempting her with a kiss that never came. On the verge of screaming out for it, the presence in her room began to make itself felt.

She blinked her eyes open, frowning at the soft light of a candle on the small half moon table by her bed. Her head turned, her heart began to race. Cole was sitting on the side of the bed watching her, his blue eyes narrowed, his muscular chest bare except for the light covering of black hair that angled down his stomach and disappeared into— Her eyes widened, then flew back to his. He was naked. Sweet God, he was naked and sporting a hard on that terrified her. Thick and long, the head purpled, the flesh heavily veined.

Tess was suddenly more than aware of her nakedness beneath the heavy quilt. When she had gone to bed, she had thought nothing of it. Now she could feel her breasts swelling, her nipples hardening. Between her legs, she felt the slow, heated moistening of her fevered flesh. She felt something else, too. Her arms were tied to the curved headboard, stretched out, the same as her legs, with very little play in the rope. Son of a bitch, he had tied her on her bed like some damned virginal sacrifice.

"What have you done?" She cleared the drowsiness from her voice as he sat still, watching her with those wicked, sensually charged eyes. "Untie me, Cole. What are you doing here?"

"First lesson," he told her, his voice soft as his lip quirked in a sexy grin. "Are you ready for it?"

"Lesson?" She shook her head, her voice filled with her surging anger. How dare the son of a bitch tie her up? "What the hell are you talking about, Cole?"

His hand lifted. Tess thought he would touch her, grab her, instead, those long fingers wrapped around his cock absently, stroking it. She swallowed tightly, her mouth watering, aching to feel that bulging head in it. She may have even considered giving into the impulse, if she could have moved her body.

"Your first lesson in being my woman, Tess," he told her, his voice cool, determined. "I told you I was tired of waiting on you. Tonight, your first lesson begins."

Tess rolled her eyes as she breathed out in irritation.

"Are you a secret psycho or something, Cole?" she bit out. "Did you just pay attention to what you said? Now let me go and stop acting so weird. Dammit, if you wanted to fuck, you should have just said so."

He smiled at her. The bastard just smiled that slow, wicked grin of his.

"But, Tess, I don't want to just fuck," he said, his voice amused. "I want you know who controls your body, your lusts. I want you to know, all the way to your soul, who owns that pretty pussy, that tempting little ass and hot mouth. I want you to admit they're mine, and mine alone to fuck however I please."

Damn. She knew Cole was into kink, but rape?

"Cole." She fought to keep her voice reasonable. "This is no way to go about getting a woman, hon. Really. You know, flowers, courtship, that's the way to a woman's heart."

"Really?" He was openly laughing at her now. "I sent you flowers, darling—"

Her eyes widened.

"Oh yeah, with a card telling me what size butt plug to buy so you could fuck my ass," she bit out as she jerked at the ropes binding her ankles. "Real romantic, Cole."

She remembered her sense of horror, the shameful excitement when she read the card. She had dumped flowers and all in the trash, but kept the card. Why, she wasn't certain.

He shrugged easily. "Practical," he told her. "I wanted you prepared. But since you were unwilling to prepare yourself, then you'll just have to accept the pain."

Pain? No. No pain.

"Now look, Cole," she warned him reasonably. "Father will be really pissed with you. And you know I'll tell—"

"I asked your father's permission first, Tess," he told her softly, his expression patient now. "Why do you think your mother finally left your father? She refused to accept who he was and what he needed. I will not make that mistake with you. You will know, and you will accept to your soul, your needs as well as my own. You won't run from me. Your father understands this, and he's giving me the time I need to help you understand."

Tess stared up at Cole, fury welling inside her as her arms jerked at the ropes that held her. Damn him, they weren't tight, but there wasn't a chance she could smack that damned superior expression off his face.

"You're lying to me," she accused him. "Father would never let you hurt me."

"Ask him in the morning." He shrugged lazily. "You'll be free by then."

A sense of impotency filled her. Damn him, he thought he had all the damned answers and all the damned plans. She wasn't a toy for him to play with, and she would show him that.

"I'll have you arrested," she promised him. "I swear, if it's the last thing I do I'll have you locked up."

He was quiet for long moments, his eyes glittering with lust, with cool knowledge.

"I wouldn't do that if I were you. And I think come morning, perhaps you will have changed your mind."

Tess breathed in hard, watching him with a sense of fear, and hating the arousal that it brought her.

"What are you talking about?" she bit out.

His hand ceased the lazy stroking of his cock, then moved to her stomach. Her muscles clenched involuntarily at the heat and calloused roughness of his flesh.

"Tonight, I'll give you a taste of what's coming," he promised her. "You'll learn, Tess, who your master is, slowly. A step at a time. Nothing too hard, baby, I promise."

Tess shivered. He didn't sound cruel, but he was determined. His voice was soft, immeasurably gentle, but filled with purpose. He would have her now, and he would have her on his terms.

"This isn't what I want, Cole," she said, fighting for breath, for a sense of control.

His hand moved lazily from her stomach, his eyes tracking each move, his fingers trailing between her thighs until one ran through the thick, slick cream that proved her words false. She trembled, biting back a moan of pleasure as the thick length of his finger dipped into her vagina.

"Isn't it?" he whispered. "I think you're lying, Tess. You shouldn't lie to me, baby."

Before Tess knew what was coming, his hand moved, then the flat of his palm delivered a stinging blow to the bare flesh of her cunt.

Tess jerked at the heat. "You son of a bitch," she screamed, jerking against her bond, ignoring the lash of pleasure that made her clit swell further. "I'll kick your ass when I get out of here."

Cole grinned, then moved from her side to position himself between her spread thighs.

"Let me go, you bastard!" she bit out, fighting to ignore the shameful pleasure and anticipation rising inside her.

"Naughty Tess," he whispered, his hand smoothing over her cunt, sliding over the moisture that lay thick and heavy on her pussy lips. "You're tight, Tess. How long has it been since you had a lover?"

"Kiss my ass!" she cried out, then jerked in surprise as his palm landed on the upper curve of her cunt. She fought the ropes, terrified of the shocking vibrations of pleasure in her clit that radiated from the heat of the blow. "Damn you!"

Her body arched as his finger slid inside her vagina once again. It was a slow stroke, the hard digit separating her muscles, making the flesh tremble in building ecstasy. She fought the need to whimper, to beg at the slow penetration.

"How long, Tess, since you've had a lover?" he asked her again.

Tess realized she was panting now, primed, ready to climax. God, if he would just let her get off.

"I hate you," she growled.

His finger stopped. Halfway inside her, her muscles clenching desperately in need, and he stopped.

"You aren't being nice, Tess," he whispered. "I could leave you tied here, hot and hurting for relief, or I could give you what you need, eventually. Now, answer my question. How long?"

The threat was clear. His finger was still inside her as he watched her, his expression hard now, though his eyes retained that lazy, gentle humor. The contrast was almost frightening.

"Four years. Satisfied—Oh God!" Her back arched, her head digging into the pillows as his finger slid home with a smooth, forceful plunge.

Tess was shuddering, her climax so close she could feel it pulsing in desperation.

"Damn you're tight, Tess." His fingertip curved, stroking the sensitive depths as she writhed against her bonds. "As tight as a virgin. I bet your ass is even tighter."

Tess stilled, quivering, seeing the lust, the excitement filling Cole's face. His cock was huge, thick and long, and she knew it would stretch her pussy until she was screaming for relief. But her ass? No way. From the look on Cole's face though, he had figured out the way of it, exactly.

Chapter 6

"Cole, let's be reasonable," Tess panted, her cunt clenching over the finger lodged inside it, quivering from the deep, gentle strokes his fingertip was administering. "Your cock will not fit there. Stop trying to scare me."

But she had a feeling it wasn't an idle threat.

He smiled. She knew better than to trust that smile. It was a slow curve of his lips, a crinkle at the corners of his eyes. Watching her carefully, he slid his finger from the soaked depths of her hot channel and then moved to lie down beside her.

Tess watched him carefully, like a wild beast as he propped his head on his arm and watched her through narrowed eyes. Then his gaze shifted, angling to her thighs, her eyes following as his hand moved.

"No—" she cried out helplessly as his hand raised.

She jerked. His head moved, his lips latching on a hard, pointed nipple a second before he delivered another stinging blow to the wet lips of her cunt.

She cried out, pleasure and pain dragging a helpless sound of confused desire from her lips as her body bowed and she jerked against him. His tongue rasped her nipple as he suckled her, and the next blow to her cunt was delivered to the flesh that shielded her swollen clit. Her cry was louder, her body jerking, arching, fighting both pain and pleasure as she struggled to separate the two. She was on fire, her head reeling from the confusing morass of sensations. She wanted to beg for more, beg for mercy.

Another blow struck her, his palm angled to deliver the blow from her clit to her vagina as he pinched her nipple between his teeth. The stinging pain, hot and fierce had her clit throbbing as she screamed from a near climax.

" Please," she begged, her head thrashing against the pillow as she felt his arm rise again. "Please, Cole — "

A strangled scream left her throat as the hardest blow landed, striking with force and fire, sending her clit blazing, her orgasm peaking against her will. It shuddered through her body as his palm ground into her clit with just enough pressure to trigger her release.

Then his lips covered hers with a groan, his tongue spearing into her mouth with greed and hunger. Tess fought to get closer, her arms and legs protesting their confinement as she met his kiss with equal voraciousness, her tongue tangling with his, her moans a harsh rasp against her throat as she felt her cunt throb, her vagina ache for more.

Tess shuddered with the throbbing intensity of her climax, a distant part of her was shocked, amazed that she could respond in such a way. Fiery tingles of sensation coursed over her body, licked at her womb, left her greedy, hungry for more. Her cunt was empty, a gnawing ache of arousal tormenting it now. It wasn't enough. She needed more. So much more.

"Do you need more, Tess??" he growled as he pulled back and stared down at her.

His eyes were no longer patient, they were hot and hungry, watching her intently.

"More. Please, Cole. I need you," she moaned staring up at him as her body moved restlessly, needing him, wanting his cock until she could barely breathe, her arousal was so intense.

He moved back, his hand going between her thighs, a ravenous groan coming from his throat as he felt the thick layer of cream that now coated her flesh.

"Your pussy's so hot, Tess." His voice sounded tortured. "So hot and sweet, I could make a meal of you now."

"Yes." She twisted against him, needing him to touch her, to fuck her, to relieve the yawning pit of exquisite need throbbing inside her.

"Not yet," he denied her, making her whimper. "Not yet, baby. But soon. Real soon."

She watched as he moved from her, going to his knees then propping her pillows beneath her shoulders and head.

"You know what I want, Tess," he told her, his voice rough, his cock aiming for her lips. "Open your mouth, baby, give me what I want."

Anything. Anything to convince him to relieve the ache that throbbed clear to her stomach. Her lips opened, and she moaned as the thick head pushed past them, stretching them wider. He was huge, so long and thick she wanted to cry out in fear, scream at him to hurry and fuck her with it.

"Oh yeah, such a hot little mouth," he groaned, wrapping his fingers around the base as he penetrated her mouth, stopping only when her eyes began to widen with the fear he would choke her. "Relax your throat, Tess," he urged her. "Just one more inch, baby. Take one more inch for me and I'll show you how good I can make you feel next."

Her pussy throbbed out her answer. *Yes, take more, bitch. Take it all so he'll fuck me.* The ravenous creature that was her cunt demanded her obedience as fiercely as Cole did. Breathing through her nose, her eyes on his, she slowly relaxed the muscles of her throat, feeling him by slow increments give her the final inch he demanded she take.

His hand tightened on his cock, his finger brushing her mouth as he marked her limit, and still there was so much more. He pulled back as Tess suckled the thick length, her tongue washing over it, rasping the underside of his dick as he nearly pulled free of her mouth until she was slurping on nothing but the engorged head, and loving it.

Then he began to penetrate again. A slow measured thrust that sank his cock to the depth he marked, his expression tightening with such extreme pleasure that she fought to caress the broad head that attempted to choke her. She let her throat make a swallowing motion, a tentative movement to test her ability to do it.

Cole groaned, his dick jerking in her mouth as he pulled back, thrust home again. She repeated the movement, watching his face, never letting go of his expression as he began to fuck her mouth. He was panting, his teeth clenched, his hard stomach clenching.

"Yes, swallow it," he growled when she repeated the motion. "Swallow it, baby. Show me you want my cock."

He was fucking her mouth harder now, her lips stretched so wide they felt bruised, but Tess loved the feeling, loved watching the excitement, the extreme lust that crossed his face each time her throat caressed the head of his cock. His hips were bucking against her, his voice a rumbled growl as he fucked her lips, pushing his cock as deep as it could go, groaning as the flesh tensed, tightened further.

"Yes. I'm going to cum now, Tess. I'm going to cum in your hot little mouth just like I'm going to cum up that tight little ass. Take it, baby, take my cock." He speared in, she swallowed, his hips jerked, then Tess felt the first hard, hot blast of his semen rocket against the back of her throat. It was followed by more. Thick hard pulses of creamy cum spurted down her throat as he cried out above her.

Tess was ecstatic, quivering with anticipation as she felt his cock, still hard, pull out of her mouth. He would fuck her now. Surely, he would fuck her now.

"You're so beautiful, Tess," he whispered as he moved away from her, staring down at her, his eyes gentle once again. "So damned hot and beautiful, you make me crazy."

"Good," she moaned. "Fuck me now, Cole. Please."

He smiled, and her eyes widened as he shook his head.

"What?" she bit out, incredulously. "Damn you, Cole, you can't leave me like this."

"Did I say I was leaving you?" he asked her, arching his brow in question. "No, Tess, I'll be here with you, all night, every night. But you're not ready to be fucked yet."

"I promise I am," she bit out. "I really am, Cole." If she got any more ready, she would go up in flames.

He chuckled, though the sound was strained.

"Not yet, Tess," he whispered. "But soon."

He moved across the room, and then Tess noticed the small tray that sat on the mantle of her wall-enclosed dresser. He picked it up and as he turned back to her, Tess's eyes widened in apprehension.

There were several sexual aids laying on the silver tray, as well as a large tube of lubrication. The one that frightened her most, was the thick butt plug that sat on its wide base. Tess trembled at the sight of it, shaking her head in fear as he neared her. If only she was frightened enough, she thought distantly. God help her, her cunt was on fire, her body so sensitive she thought a soft breeze would send her into climax. And seeing those toys, the thick butt plug and the large dildo, had her trembling, not just in fear, but in excitement.

He set the tray on her nightstand, then sat on her bed, staring at it.

"If you don't stay aroused, needing me and what I'll give you, then I'll walk away," he said, his voice so soft she had to strain to hear it. "But I'll push you, Tess, see what you like, see what you can take. Not just tonight, but all week. You're mine until the night of your father's party. No matter what, no matter when, as long as what I'm doing arouses you."

"And if it doesn't?" she asked angrily. "What are you going to do, hurt me until I can't take it anymore?"

He turned to her, his eyes blazing.

"Only I can give you what you want, what you need," he bit out. "You're so damned hot to be dominated you can't stand it. Do you think I don't know that? Did you think you were told the rumors of my preferences needlessly? If you weren't excited by it, Tess, you wouldn't have been so wet you soaked my hand two years ago when I caught you in the hall. You're just scared of it. And I want you too damned bad to let you stay frightened of what we both need any longer."

"I won't do it!" But excitement was electrifying her body, making every cell throb in anticipation.

"Won't you?" he growled. "I know about the books your mother found in your room when you went to college, Tess. The stories you read, to satisfy that craving you couldn't explain."

Her face flushed. Her mother had been enraged over the naughty books she had found in Tess's room that year.

"Captives, dominated by their lovers. Submissive, loving every stroke of the sensual pleasure they received.

Tess could feel her flush of mortification staining her entire body.

"Did you ever fuck your ass, Tess?" he asked her softly, leaning toward her, watching her closely. "As you stroked your cunt, fighting for orgasm, did your finger ever steal into that hot, dark little passage, just to see what it felt like?"

She had. Tess moaned in humiliation. But it hadn't been her finger, rather it had been the rounded, slender vibrator she kept hidden. The dark surge of pleasure that had spread through her had been terrifying. Even worse had been the hard, shocking quake of an orgasm that had her nearly screaming, ripping through her body, and making her cunt gush its slick, sticky fluid. The remembered pain of the penetration, the humiliation of that rushing liquid squirting from her had caused her to never try such a thing again except with her fingers. Even now, years later, the thought of that one act was enough to leave her flushing with shame.

"Did it hurt, Tess?" And of course, those wicked eyes knew the flush of admission on her skin. "Did it make you want more?"

"No," she bit out, shaking with nerves, with arousal.

"I think it did." He touched her cheek, his fingers caressing her flesh, his voice gentle. "I think I left you aching, needing, and too damned scared to try to reach for it. I think, Tess, that you need me just as much as I need you."

"And I think you're crazy," she bit out, refusing him, wondering why she was when she needed it so damned bad.

His thumb stroked over her swollen lips, his eyes dark, glittering in the light of the candle.

"Am I?" he asked her softly. "Let's see, Tess, just how crazy I am."

Chapter 7

Tess watched Cole, trying to still the hard, rough breaths that shook her body. She couldn't seem to get enough oxygen, couldn't seem to settle the hard shudder of her pounding heart.

"There's a fine line that divides pleasure and pain," he told her as he removed the butt plug from the tray, and the tube of lubricant. "It's so slim, that if went about the right way, the pain adds to the pleasure, in a dark erotic manner."

He moved to the bottom of the bed. He loosened the ropes attached to the footboard, then grabbed her legs quickly before she could kick out at him. Ignoring her struggles and heated curses, within minutes he had her entire body flipped over, the ropes once again holding her in position as he tucked several pillows beneath her hips.

"You bastard." Her voice was strangled as crazed excitement shot through her body.

Her buttocks were arched to him now. She was spread, open to him, and the flares of fear and excitement traveling through her body had her terrified.

"God, Tess, you're beautiful," he growled from behind her, his voice rough, filled with lust. "Your little ass so pink and pretty. And I like how you keep your pussy waxed so soft and smooth. But I would have preferred to do it myself. From now on, I'll take care of it for you."

Tess trembled, crying out. She should hate this. She should be screaming, begging him to stop, instead her body pulsed in need and desire, in anticipation.

"You shouldn't have waited so long to come back, Tess," he whispered as he kissed one full cheek of her ass. "You shouldn't have made me wait so long, baby, because I won't be able to be as gentle as I would have been."

Her cunt pulsed at his words.

"And I'll have to punish you." She whimpered at the rising excitement in his voice. "But I would have anyway, Tess. Because I need to see that pretty ass all red and hot from my hand."

"No—" Despite her instinctive cry, his hand fell to the rounded cheek of her ass.

Heat flared across her flesh, then she screamed as his finger sank into her pussy a second later. She twisted, writhed against her bonds.

"You're so wet," he groaned. "So tight and hot, Tess. But by the time my cock sinks into your pretty pussy, you'll be tighter."

His hand struck again as the broad finger retreated from her quaking vagina. As the heat built in the flesh of her buttocks, his finger sank in again. Tess was crying out in fear and a wash of dark, erotic excitement. The blows weren't cruel, rather sharp and stinging, building a steady heat in her flesh.

"So pretty." He whacked the other side, then his finger thrust into her again.

She was so wet she was dripping. He alternated mild and stinging blows that kept her flinching in anticipation. Kept her flesh heated, the pain flaring through her body. A pain she hated, hated because the pleasure from it was driving her crazy. She could feel her juices rolling from her cunt, hear her cries echoing with needs she didn't want to name.

By the time he finished, her ass felt on fire, her hips were rolling, her cunt throbbing. She was dying of need. If he didn't fuck her soon, she would go crazy. She was burning, inside and out, a wave of fiery lust tormenting her loins as she fought the depraved pleasures of the spanking.

"Your ass is so pretty and red now," he groaned. "Damn, Tess, I like you like this, baby, all tied up for me, reddening, your cunt hot and tight and so wet it soaks my fingers." Two fingers plunged inside her.

"Cole—" Her cry was hoarse and desperate as her orgasm teetered her on an edge of agonized excitement.

"I'm going to put this butt plug up your ass now, Tess," he warned her as he drew his fingers from her body. "Then I'll fuck you, baby. I'll fuck you so deep and hard you won't ever leave me again."

Tess's head ground into her pillow as his hand separated her buttocks. She flinched at the feel of cold lubricant, then cried out again as his finger sank fully into the tight hole. It pinched, sent a flare of heat through her muscles that had her bucking into the thrust.

"Oh, Tess, your ass is so tight." He twisted his finger inside her, spreading the lubrication, stretching the muscles as she whimpered in distress. "It doesn't want to stretch, Tess. Such a pretty virgin hole."

As full as his finger filled her, how would she ever take more? She tightened on him in fear, then moaned as the heated pain made her cunt throb hotter. She was depraved. She should be terrified, fighting him, instead her whimpers were begging for more.

He repeated the lubrication several times as Tess fought to breathe past the pleasure and pain. She was ready to scream, to beg for more. She wanted to whisper the forbidden words. She bit her lip, panted, cried out as his finger finally withdrew.

"Tess, I want you to take a deep breath," he finally instructed her heatedly. "Relax when the plug starts in, it will ease the pain if it's too much for you at first."

"You're torturing me," she cried out, bucking against her ropes. She didn't want this now. She was too scared. The dark lust rolling over her was too intense, too frightening. "Stop, Cole. Let me go!"

"It's okay, Tess." His hand smoothed over her bottom then his fingers clenched, separating her again. "It's okay, baby. It's normal to be scared. Just relax."

"Cole—" She didn't know if her cry was in protest or in need as she felt the tapered head of the thick plug nestle against her tiny hole.

"It's going to hurt, Tess." His voice was dark, excited. "You're going to scream for me, and you're going to love it. I know you will, baby."

"Oh God." She tossed her head on the pillow but couldn't help allowing her body to relax marginally.

She felt the device begin to penetrate the tight hole. At first, the piercing sensation was mild, but as the length and thickness increased, the steady, building fire began to shoot through her body.

She tensed, but Cole didn't ease up. She cried out as it grew brighter, then began begging as pain bloomed in her anus. But she wasn't begging him to stop.

"It hurts," she screamed out. "Oh God, Cole. Cole please—"

He didn't relent, instead, the fingers of his other hand moved to her pulsing cunt. There, they stroked and petted her clit until she was thrusting, pushing into his hand, crying out as the movement pushed the plug deeper into her ass.

She could feel her muscles stretching, protesting but eventually giving way to the thick intruder invading it. She bucked against her ropes, rearing back, writhing under the lash of burning pain, and equally burning pleasure.

"Damn you!" Her voice was hoarse, enraged from the building kaleidoscope of sensations rushing through her body.

The fiery heat of the invasion, the slow steady buildup of pain, the resulting agonizing pleasure so overwhelmed her senses that she felt dazed with it, awash in a darkly sensual reality where nothing existed except the slow, steady invasion of her ass, and the soft, too light caresses to her throbbing clit.

Long minutes later she jerked harshly as the last inch of the plug passed the tight anal ring, leaving seven inches of hard thick dildo lodged inside her. She squirmed, fighting to accustom herself to the sensation. Cole chose that moment to land his hand heavily on her ass again. Tess screamed, her muscles tightening around the plug, inflicting a disastrous form of ecstasy.

"Now, Tess," Cole growled. "Now, I get to eat that pretty pussy."

Chapter 8

Tess's cries were echoing in his head, throbbing in his cock. Cole couldn't remember a time he had been so turned on, so hot and ready to fuck. He wanted to plunge his cock as deep, as hard up her tight cunt as he could. He wanted to slam it inside her, master her with the brutality of a fucking so lustful that she would find it impossible to leave the only man who could give it to her.

But he knew, the longer he could keep her hanging on the edge of the sensations ripping through her, the more she would crave it later. He was a slave to the need to be the one who pleasured her.

The piercing of her ass with that plug had been the most erotic, satisfying thing he had done in his life. He wondered if she was even aware of how loud she had begged for more. How many times she had pleaded with him to push it hard inside her, to take her. He doubted it. Submissives rarely remembered that first time, those first long minutes that the plug, or a hot, thick cock invaded their ass.

It was the pain and pleasure combined. The needs, so shocking, so consuming that they dazed the mind to the point that the submissive rarely remembered begging for it.

"Fuck me," Tess still begged, her voice was thick and desperate as her cunt leaked the honeyed cream of her need. And he would fuck her. Soon.

He lifted a small, oblong metal device from the tray. It was attached to a long cord with a control box at the end.

A silver bullet it was called. So tiny it appeared harmless, but the effects of its internal vibrations would send Tess into such a haze of rapture that she would never forget it.

He inserted the three-inch long device into her cunt. His cock clenched at the closed fist tightness he encountered as he pressed it past the fullness of the plug lodged in her ass and moved it to the back of her cunt. He positioned the little device for maximum vibration against her G-spot then withdrew. He set the control on low, a gentle, stroking vibration that nonetheless caused her to flinch. Then he set about feeding himself from her cunt.

He lapped at her pussy, just as he had once promised her he would. Gentle strokes into her vagina with his tongue that had her bucking against his mouth, begging for more. Her body was sheened with sweat, her breathing harsh, her cries desperate as he tongued her, stroked her. And she tasted so damned good he couldn't help himself but to thrust his tongue as deep inside her as he could go, and draw more of her into his mouth.

Cole was on fire for her. He knew his control was slipping, something that never happened, something he had never had to fight to keep before. But he had to prepare her, he couldn't allow himself to unwittingly hurt her. Tess was everything to him. His heart, his soul, the happiness he had always believed he would never find. She teetered between erotic pain and the pain that could irrevocably damage her sexuality forever. If he wasn't careful, extremely careful, then he would destroy both of them. Because Cole knew he couldn't go much longer without her.

So he tamped down his own lusts, stroked her gently, gauged her need and advanced the speed of the vibrator accordingly. She was bucking in his hands now, nearing that point of no return. Reluctantly, he moved back from her dripping vagina, licked back, circled her clit with his tongue. Then he turned, laying on his back, positioning himself to suck the swollen, engorged bud into his mouth as he edged the speed of the vibrator higher.

She exploded, her body tensed. Her scream was strangled, breathless as her body bowed, jerked, then began a repeated shudder that signaled the beginning of her orgasm. He tightened his lips on her clit, flicked it with his tongue and held her hips with easy strength when the hot, volcanic rush of her release began to rush through her body.

* * * * *

Tess was dying. She knew she was dying and she eagerly embraced the exquisite rush of painful pleasure that threw her over the brink. Her body was jerking uncontrollably, her orgasm filling her body, pumping through her blood, spasming her uterus as it tore through her. She could feel the hard vibration inside her, Cole's lips at her clit, blending into a raging storm she knew she wouldn't survive. Hard shudders rushed over her, pleasure, unlike anything she could have conceived tore her apart. And in a distant part of her mind, she wondered if she would ever be the same again. If she survived it.

She screamed against the torrent, but couldn't fight it. She could feel her fluids gushing through her pussy as it spasmed, and Cole's mouth moving to catch them with a hard, male groan. His tongue speared inside her tortured cunt, triggering another hard shudder, another gush of fluids until finally, she collapsed mindlessly against her ropes, dazed, stripped of strength.

Small tremors still assaulted her boneless body. The never-ending pulse of her climax didn't go away easily. She could hear Cole, a hard, brutal male groan echoing through the room as his body jerked against her. Had he come? Had he been inside her and she didn't know it? It didn't matter. She was drifting on a haze of pleasure so weak, so astounding that she couldn't think, and didn't want to.

"Tess?" Cole's voice was tender, warm as he moved behind her. "Are you okay, baby?"

She felt the ropes loosening, his hands calloused and gentle on her skin as he untied her, helped her to stretch out on the bed. She lay boneless, so satiated she could barely move. She was aware of Cole moving along the bed beside her, turning her over to her back, his expression, when she looked up at him, was concerned, gentle.

"Sleepy," she whispered. And she was. So tired, so emotionally and physically drained she could barely stay awake.

"Sleep, Tess." He kissed her cheek gently. "Rest, baby. We start again tomorrow."

* * * * *

Cole lay down beside her, drawing the quilt over them, ignoring the pulse of his still throbbing cock. He had climaxed with Tess, but it wasn't enough. He needed to be buried inside her, feeling her, tight and hot, enclosing him with her satin heat.

And he knew the fight wasn't finished. Accepting the pain-filled pleasure would be the easy part for Tess. Submitting to him would be the hard part. Giving in to him, no matter what he asked of her, no matter what he demanded for her sexual pleasure, would be the fight. One he looked forward to. He knew Tess better than she knew herself. He knew from her father's admission of the books her mother had found, what turned her on. It wasn't the pain, it was the domination, the submission into the sexual extremes that she craved. She wanted to fight. She wanted to be vanquished, and he wanted to give it to her.

He pulled her against him, luxuriating in the warmth of her body, her very presence. He had dreamed of this for two years. He knew the moment he met Tess that she held a part of him that no other woman ever could. The thought of it had tormented him, racked him with lust. In the past months, it had grown worse. He lived and breathed daily with the need for her. It was like a fever burning his loins that he couldn't escape.

And now he had her. By Valentine's night, her final lesson, her final erotic dream fulfilled, she would know who mastered her body and her heart.

Chapter 9

Tess was sore. Her entire body throbbed, protesting her wakefulness. The muscles of her legs were stiff and burning, her arms and even her breasts were sore.

"Open your eyes, Tess. We have to remove the plug and you need a hot bath." Cole's voice was firm, brooking no refusal.

Her eyes snapped open, her head turning to him, her eyes focusing on the savage features of his face.

"You left that thing in me?" she bit out incredulously.

He arched a single brow.

"Your ass was tight, Tess. It needs to accustom itself to stretching before you'll ever be able to take my cock there."

Her heart slammed into her ribs.

"Go to the bathroom, then come back here. If you try to remove it yourself, I'll tie you back down and leave you there the rest of the day."

He meant it. She saw his determination in the hard lines of his face.

"Take it out first," she said instead.

He shook his head. "Do as I say, Tess. I have a reason for my demands, baby."

Tess frowned, but she knew she did not want to experience the torture of being tied down and frothing with need. And she knew he would make her froth. He would torture her, then leave her to suffer in her arousal. She wasn't ready to take that chance yet, not after last night.

So she rose from the bed, walking gingerly to the bathroom. After relieving her most pressing need, she brushed her teeth and washed her face then returned to the bedroom. Her stomach rolled with nerves, wondering how Cole planned to continue the sensual torture he had started last night.

"On your knees." He nodded to the bed, standing beside it, naked and sporting an erection that resembled a weapon.

His cock was the largest she had ever seen, nearly as thick as her wrist, with a bulging, flared head that made her mouth water at the sight.

Tess went to the bed, assuming the position she knew he wanted. She trembled as his hand caressed the cheeks of her rear. His fingers ran down the crease of her ass until he gripped the plug, pulling it slowly, gently, free of her bottom.

"Stay still," he ordered her before she could move. "Under your cabinet are some personal supplies I bought for you. From now on you will use them whenever I tell you to do so. Understood?"

"Yes," she whispered, feeling her cunt burn, moisten as he ran his hands over her ass.

"I'm not going to fuck you now because to be honest, I don't think I can keep my cock out of your ass. But I need relief, baby."

He moved around the bed then, turning her as he faced her, his cock aiming at her mouth. Tess licked her lips. She opened them as the purpled head nudged against them. She heard his hard groan as she closed her lips around his cock, taking him, opening her throat to take that last inch possible.

One of his hands gripped his cock, to assure he didn't give her more than she could take, the other twisted in her hair. The sharp bite of pain had her mouth tightening around his cock, her throat working on the head as he cried out in pleasure. He wasn't willing to prolong his own pleasure this morning though. His thrust in and out of her mouth with deep, hard strokes, holding her still as he groaned repeatedly at the pleasure she was bringing him. Then, she felt his cock jerk, throb, and the pulse of his sperm filling her mouth as he cried out his release.

Cole was breathing hard when he pulled back from her, his cock was still engorged, still ready for her, but he did nothing more.

"Go bathe, Tess, before I do something neither of us is ready for. Come down to breakfast when you're finished."

Tess stood up, watching him fight for control.

"Is Father home?" she asked

"Not yet." He shook his head. "He'll be back the night before the party. You're mine until then, Tess. Can you handle it?"

Her eyes narrowed at his tone of voice, the suggestion that she couldn't.

"I can handle you any day of the week." Damn her mouth, she groaned as the words poured from her lips.

His lips quirked. They both knew better.

"We'll see." He nodded. "Go bathe. I'll lay out what I want you to wear this morning. The servants have been given the rest of the week off as well, so there's just you and me for a while."

Tess bit her lip. She wasn't certain if that was a good thing or not.

"Go." He indicated the bathroom door. "Come downstairs when you're ready."

* * * * *

An hour later Tess walked down the spiraling stairs, barefoot and wearing more clothes than she thought he would lay out for her but decidedly less than she wanted to wear. The long, silk negligee made her feel sexy, feminine. It covered her breasts but was cut low enough that if he wanted them out, he would have no problems. There were no panties included, but the black silk shielded that fact. She would have been uncomfortable in something he could have seen right through.

His note had stated that he would await her in the kitchen, and there he was. Dressed in sweat pants and nothing else, his thick black hair still damp, looking sexier than any man had a right to look. And he was smiling at her. Even his eyes were filled with a lazy, comfortable expression as he set two plates of eggs, bacon and toast beside full coffee cups.

"Breakfast is ready, you're right on time." He pulled her chair out, indicating that she should sit.

Tess took her seat gingerly, the soreness of her muscles was much better, but her thighs and rear were still tender.

"Sore?" He brushed a kiss over her bare shoulder, causing her to jerk in startled reaction.

She turned her head, looking up at him as he straightened and moved to his own chair.

"A little." She cleared her throat.

"It will get easier," he promised. "Now eat. We'll talk later, after you've been fed."

Breakfast, despite her initial misgivings, was filled with laughter. Cole was comfortable and his easy humor began to show. His dry wit kept her chuckling and the wicked sparkle in his eyes kept her body sizzling, kept her anticipating later, praying he would fuck her. The longer he waited, the hotter she got. She didn't know if she would survive it much longer.

Finally, after the dishes were finished, he drew her through the house into the comfortable living room. A fire crackled in the corner of the room where a large, thick pillow mattress had been laid.

"Sit down, we need to talk." He drew her down on the mattress, then onto her back as he lay beside her.

"Look, I don't much feel like talking," she finally said in frustration. "Let's just cut to the chase here, Cole. There are things I evidently like, that you enjoy doing. I don't want to talk about them. Just do them."

She stared up at him, narrowing her eyes, warning him that she too had her limits.

He propped his head on his hand, regarding her with a curious expression.

"I expected more of a fight," he said, a vague question in his voice.

Tess sighed, sitting up staring into the fire as she ran the fingers of one hand through her hair.

"How extreme do you intend to get?" she finally asked him, glancing at him as he still reclined beside her.

He reached over, his fingers trailing down her hair. "How extreme do you want me to get, Tess?" he asked instead. "I can give you whatever you want, anything you want. But I have my own needs, and they will have to be satisfied as well."

"Such as?" she asked him, keeping her voice low, stilling the tremor that threatened to shake it.

"I like the toys, Tess. I like using them, and I'm dying to use them on you. I like spanking you. I like watching your pretty pussy and the rounded cheeks of your ass turning red. I like hearing you scream because you don't know if it hurts or if it's the pleasure killing you. I want to see your eyes filled with dazed pleasure as I push your limits." He laid it out for her pretty well, she thought with an edge of silent mockery, and still didn't answer a damned thing.

"How far will you go?" she asked him.

"How far will you let me go?" he countered her.

Tess had a feeling she would have few limits, but she wasn't willing to tell him that.

"You evidently have plans. I'd like to know what they are."

Cole sighed. "Some things are better left up to the pleasure of the moment. Let's wait and see what happens."

Tess licked her lips in nervousness. Evidently her father had told him about the debacle with the books her mother had found. He wouldn't have known about them otherwise. She took a deep, hard breath.

"Does it concern other men?" she finally asked.

His eyes lit up in arousal. Tess lowered her head to her knees. God, she didn't know if she could.

"You want it, Tess." He moved behind her, sitting up to pull her against him as he whispered the words in her ear. "You've wanted it for a long time, baby, everything I have planned. Just settle down, and we'll take it step by step."

Tess was fighting to control her breathing, her heart rate. She was terrified of him, and of herself.

"I can't, if Father found out—"

"Tess, your father knows," he said gently. "Why do you think your mother divorced him? She didn't want sex, let alone what he needed. Your father knew when those books were found what you needed. Just as he knows what I need."

Embarrassment coursed through her body. She remembered coming home from college, her mother raging at her, the humiliation of the accusations she had thrown at Tess. It was one of the few times her father had put his foot down. Then he had pulled her into his study and uncomfortably informed her that sexuality was a personal thing, and none of his or her mother's business.

"Your sister — ?" She left the question hanging.

"Knows what he wants and enjoys it. That's the key point, Tess. You have to enjoy it, otherwise, it brings me no pleasure. Your pleasure is most important, Tess. What you want, what you need."

His hands were at her abdomen, softly stroking the nervous muscles there. His lips brushed over her shoulder, her neck.

"I don't want a toy, Tess," he promised her. "Or a woman who doesn't know her mind and speak up accordingly. But in the bedroom, that is where I want the woman I know you are. If you want to fight me, then fight. If you want to submit, then do so. If you want to be tied down and raped, let me know. All of it, I can give you and enjoy. But if you ever reach a limit, you have to tell me. If I ever suggest something you don't want or can't handle, then you have to speak up. And after that, unless you ask for it, it will never be approached again. So be very careful in the pleasures you deny yourself."

She lifted her head from her knees.

"And when you're tired of me?" she asked him.

"What if you grow tired of me first?" he asked her then. "It goes both ways, Tess. If we can't give the other what they need, then there's no point in going on. Do you agree?"

Her hands clenched at her knees. "I agree," she whispered.

"There are no rules, Tess. But from this point on, no means no. If you don't want it, then you say the word. Understand?"

She nodded nervously.

"Each night, I'll push you further. Each night, you'll learn something new about yourself." His hands moved to her arms, caressing the tight muscles, easing the nervousness locking them up. "Don't be frightened of me, Tess. Or of yourself."

"No other women." She wanted it clear from the beginning. "I don't know if I can even handle another man. But you can have no other women."

"I don't want another woman, Tess," he assured her. "And there will be no other men, unless it's something I decide." His voice hardened. "There is a particular pleasure in sharing your woman that you may never understand. But not just any man would be worthy of the privilege, baby, trust me."

"If you don't fuck me now, I'll walk out of this house and I won't come back," she finally breathed roughly. "I'm tired of waiting, Cole."

She had turned the tables on him then, she moved before he could stop her, turning and pressing against his shoulders until he lay back on the mattress. He was already hard, and she was already wet. His cock tented the front of his pants, hiding him from her. Hooking her hands in the waistband she pulled them down, lifting them over the thick erection and jerking them from his legs.

"I wondered when you would get tired of waiting," he said with a smile, though his gaze was hot, wickedly lustful.

Tess jerked the gown over her head, then moved up his body. She heard his hard breath when her damp cunt grazed his cock, but she continued on. She wanted his kiss. She was dying for it.

As her lips touched his, his arms went around her, turning her, flipping her onto her back as he rose above her. His tongue pierced her mouth, his lips slanting over hers as he turned the caress into a carnal feast. Tess moaned brokenly, feeling the tenderness, the utter warmth of his touch, his body above hers, the easy strength of his muscles as he kept her close against him.

"My dick is so hard I won't last five minutes inside you," he bit out. "Are you on the pill, or do I need a condom?"

"Pill," she gasped. She didn't want anything between them. She wanted to feel him when he came, feel his seed spurting hard inside her.

"Damn, Tess, I'm almost scared to fuck you, you're so damned tight," he growled as his hand smoothed over her cunt, his finger testing her vagina.

Tess arched into the penetration, her hungry moan shocking her as her body begged for more.

His lips trailed along her neck, moving steadily down, down to the hard, sensitive tips of her breasts. When his mouth covered one, her womb contracted painfully. Oh yeah. That was good. SO good. His tongue rasped over the tip, his mouth suckling at her with a strong motion that left her quivering. Then he nibbled at the small bud, the slight pinch driving her arousal higher with the edge of pain.

"Damn, you're so hot you're burning me alive," he growled, moving back to her lips, searing them with his kiss.

"Burn more then," she panted. "Please, Cole. Take me now."

He rose above her moving between her thighs, spreading them wide, as she watched his cock pulse.

"It might hurt," he warned her, breathing heavy. "Damn, Tess, I've never had a pussy so tight it burned my finger before."

She rolled her hips, tormented by the tip of his cock as it nudged against her vagina.

"That's okay," she whimpered. " You can handle it."

He surged inside her.

The breath left Tess's body as it bowed, a strangled scream tearing from her throat at the forced separation of her sensitive vaginal muscles. The burning pleasure/pain consumed her, traveling through her as she twisted against the thick cock lodged in her cunt.

"Sweet mercy, Tess," Cole cried out as he came over her heavily, his elbows bracing to take his weight. His hips rolled in a smooth motion between her thighs that sent sharp darts of ecstasy traveling through her body.

* * * * *

He wasn't going to last long. Cole knew he didn't have a prayer of it. The best he could hope for was that Tess wouldn't either. He grabbed her hips, his face buried in the damp curve of her neck as he began a strong steady motion inside her body.

Her cunt was so tight it burned, so slick and sweet he could stay inside her forever if only he could hold his release back that long. There wasn't a chance. She twisted against him, her hips lifting for him, her legs wrapping around his waist as she took him deeper, screaming out with the sensations his hard thrusts sent through her.

Cole groaned at her heat. He pushed into her harder, his thrusts gaining in speed, spearing inside her, sliding through sensitive tissue that gripped him, fought to hold him. Her body tightened further until finally, her pussy began to quake around him as she cried out, jerking in his arms, her orgasm slamming into her at the same time he lost control.

Cole heard his howl of ecstasy, her strangled scream of release as he began spurting inside her. Heat enveloped him, seared him, filled his body and soul as her hold on him tightened.

"Tess. God, Tess, baby—" He didn't think the hard flares of pleasure would ever end. Prayed they never did. They shot up his spine, through his dick, and dissolved the hard, lonely core to his heart. This woman was his. And before the week was over, he would prove it to her.

Chapter 10

For Tess, the days continued in a haze of pleasure. Cole was alternately gentle and masterful, seductive and surprising. He pushed her as he warned he would. He tied her down and tormented her with his skillful tongue and a variety of sexual toys meant to both tease and torment. Throughout the day she wore the silky gowns he laid out for her, and roamed the house with him. They talked and laughed, made love and lust in a variety of rooms and positions. But more importantly, Tess learned about the man.

The privileged, driven man whose incredible intelligence often hid a man of intense emotions. She would catch glimpses of it during certain conversations or after a session of intense, almost brutal lovemaking. His expression would be concerned, loving, as though despite his needs, his desires, he feared hurting her.

He still made her wear the butt plug for several hours daily. Before it was time to remove it, he would fuck her slow and easy, his cock sliding forcefully inside the ultra tight passage of her vagina. The sensation was incredible. Tess would scream for him, beg, plead for mercy as the streaking pain and pleasure assaulted her body. Her climaxes tore her body apart with the sensations, leaving her heaving against him, her juices exploding around his cock and triggering his own climax.

Their time was slowly coming to a close, though. On the sixth day, Tess dressed in yet another gown. The new one was a Grecian design that fell to her feet, with small golden silken ropes crossing over the front from her abdomen to beneath her breasts. She was barefoot again, but she knew that Cole would be as well. He wore clothes easy to remove. She grinned. For the most part, they went naked through the house anyway.

They went through breakfast quickly. Tess knew Cole had something planned for the day, but she wasn't certain what. She learned quickly a bit later, though. As she lay on the mattress in front of the fire Cole pulled four massively heavy weights from the corner of the room. He placed one at each corner of the mattress, then gave her that dark, commanding look that set her blood on fire.

"Last lesson," he whispered, tying a length of silken rope on the metal rings wielded to them. "Take off your gown and lay on your stomach."

A tremor of arousal shook her body as she pulled the gown from her body. Cole then buckled a leather band at each ankle and wrist before attaching the ropes to them. It left her spread, defenseless, with just enough play in the rope for him to place large, wide pillows beneath her body, levering her several inches above the mattress. Under her hips he placed yet another, leaving her ass defenseless, open to his gaze.

"Who owns your body?" he whispered, running his finger along the flaming crease of her cunt as his other hand stroked her buttocks.

"I do." Her voice was rough. She was in the right position for punishment; she didn't want to waste it.

His hand landed on her ass with stinging force. She flinched, cried out at the flare of heat in her flesh and deep within her cunt.

"Who owns your body, Tess?" he asked her again.

"Not you," she cried out. She needed more, again. She wanted him to set her ass to burning, because she knew what it would do to the rest of her body. Her breasts were swollen, her nipples hard and hurting.

He slapped her again.

"Who owns your body?"

"Me." The haze of arousal was dulling reality now. His hand landed again.

"Need any help, Cole?" For a moment, Tess thought she imagined the smooth, cultured voice coming from the doorway.

She opened her eyes, her head turning, her eyes widening in mortification at the man leaning casually against the doorframe.

Jesse Wyman was one of the vice presidents at her father's company, answerable only to Cole and her father. He was as darkly handsome as Cole was, but more refined, not as large or savage looking. His green eyes were dark now, filled with lust rather than calculation, and the bulge in his pants looked more than impressive.

"Cole?" Was this part of his plan, if not, her suddenly dripping pussy may just get her into trouble.

"Say no and he walks away." Cole's voice was hot, suggestive. "Do you remember the book your mother threw the biggest fit over, Tess?" he whispered hotly. "The woman was tied down, her ass raised, her cunt, her mouth and her ass at the mercy of the hero and his best friend? Meet my best friend, baby."

Tess quivered. She could feel Cole's hand stroking over her heated bottom, Jesse's eyes following the caress. Her heart labored heavily in excitement, the blood thundering through her veins. She had always wondered what it would feel like. Wondered if she could handle two men at once.

"Cole—?" She was frightened too. The unfamiliar longings were shuttling through her body, making her shake in indecision.

"Tess, " he whispered. "It won't be the last time I ask it of you. I promise you, baby, you'll love it."

She could hear the excitement in his voice, the arousal as Jesse started into the room, his hands going to the buttons of his white dress shirt.

"God, you two do this all the time?" she gasped.

"Just sometimes. Just when it's important, Tess. When we know it's needed. And baby, you need it." His finger dipped into her pussy, pushing through the frothing juice that dripped from it.

Tess groaned, pushing back into his finger as Jesse dropped his shirt to the floor. His chest was muscular and deeply tanned. His green eyes glittering with rising lust. Tess watched, mesmerized as his hand went to the fastening of his slacks.

"She's beautiful," Jesse growled as he kicked his shoes off then disposed of his slacks and boxers. "Has she been a good girl for you, Cole?" His voice was suggestive, searing her with the implication that she needed to be punished.

His hands tested the restraints at her wrists, then his fingers feathered over her cheek. Tess shuddered at the caress.

"Tess usually finds a way to be naughty, don't you, baby?" Cole's hand landed on her bottom in a light smack.

She jerked, whimpering. Dear God, they were both going to punish her, pleasure her? She felt faint from excitement, her body tingling. She nearly climaxed when Jesse came to his knees beside her, his erection not as large as Cole's, but nearly. It was thick, pulsing, the head throbbing. His hand touched her hair, his eyes locked with hers, and then Tess understood why Cole had propped pillows beneath her whole body. To raise her high enough to keep her arms stretched wide, and still in position for any cock sucking required. Her mouth watered at the thought, then opened in a cry of surprise when Cole's hand struck her ass again.

"Naughty Tess." His voice was filled with amusement.

"Beautiful Tess," Jesse's voice was a low growl of pleasure. "Her butt pinkens so well. Does it stretch as easily?"

"My ass," Cole grunted. "I haven't fucked it yet, so you can't either."

Jesse grunted but said nothing more. A second later, Tess felt his lips at her shoulder, his teeth scraping over her skin as his hands reached beneath her on either side to cup her full, swollen breasts. His fingers gripped her nipples, pinching lightly as she groaned at the hot little flare of pain. She jerked at the caress, fighting to breathe as she felt Cole's hand descend on her ass once again. She was bucking at each blow, crying out as Jesse alternately soothed and inflamed her nipples, his mouth on her neck, nibbling, licking at her, keeping her poised on a pinnacle of arousal so sharp it was agony.

It was then that Tess felt Cole move away from her for a second. When he returned, his finger, thickly lubricated, began to work its way up her still tight anus. He slid the first in easily, though her muscles pinched at the entrance. He pulled back slowly, then two broad fingers were working up the tight channel, spreading her, thrusting lightly inside as she cried out, begging for more.

Jesse's fingers tightened on her nipples, then caressed them, tightened again, caressed again. Cole's fingers, three now, worked slowly up her small back entrance, his voice hot and encouraging as she opened to him, her muscles stretching as it sent fire flaring through her body.

"I'm going to fuck your ass today, Tess," he growled. "I'm going to lubricate you real good, baby, then I'm going to work my cock up your tight ass and listen to you scream for me. Will you scream for me, baby?"

Scream? She couldn't breathe. She was gasping for breath as Jesse pulled the pillows from beneath her body, lying down beside her, his strong arms holding her up as he pushed his head under her to catch a hard, turgid nipple in his mouth.

There was enough slack to the ropes holding her wrists now that she could partially prop herself up with her hands. Jesse helped her hold her weight, splayed as she was, with his hard hands beneath her breasts. But did little for her strength. The strong suction, strong nips and rasping tongue on her tender nipples were driving her crazy.

Her head tossed as she panted for breath. Cole's fingers were working further up her ass now, spilling fire and hot, dark rapture as he slowly stretched her, his fingers spreading inside her to part the heated passage.

"Jesse is going to fuck your tight pussy for me, Tess," Cole promised her, his voice rough from his lust. "After I work my cock up your sweet ass, he's going to take that tight cunt. You'll be stretched and full baby, both of us working you, fucking you."

His explicit words caused her womb to spasm painfully, her body to bow involuntarily as she pushed against his fingers.

"Oh yes, baby, you want it, don't you?" Pleasure filled his voice. "You want to be taken, filled and fucked like the sweet treasure you are."

His voice was awed, enraptured, as though it were she giving him a gift, rather than the other way around. As Cole spoke, Jesse pushed his body beneath hers, sliding easily in the space the cushions had once taken until she was draped over him, his cock nestling at the soaked lips of her bare cunt.

"Tess, I wish you could see how beautiful you look," Cole groaned as he moved back until Jesse could get into position. "Your sweet cunt is dripping all over his cock, soaking it. Your ass raised and ready for me. Are you ready for me, baby?"

Tess whimpered. Was she ready? The thought of his cock, so thick and hard pushing up her ass was at once terrifying and exhilarating.

"I think you're ready." She felt him move into position as Jesse reached around, pulling the cheeks of her ass apart.

"Relax for me, Tess," Cole groaned. "I promise, it's gonna be so good."

She felt the head of his cock begin its entrance inside her. Slowly, easing inside her, stretching her until she was screaming out at the shocking pain of the entrance. Pain and pleasure, it seared her, held her immobile as he worked his cock inside her, inch by inch.

Jesse held her flesh apart, but his lips caressed her face, whispering encouragement, dark, naughty words that made her need for the sexual pain flare higher, hotter. His voice was approving, tender.

"It's okay, Tess," he soothed her as she bucked, her eyes tearing from the pain, though she didn't want it to stop. She never wanted it to stop. "Don't fight it, Tess," he urged. "Cole's cock is thick, baby, but not too thick. You can take it." He pulled her flesh apart further, easing the shocking pain as Cole continued to tunnel inside her.

"Tess, are you okay, baby?" She could hear the strain in his voice, the hot vibrating vein of lust and possession, caring and tenderness.

"Please—" she gasped as he halted the slow, gliding entrance.

The head of his cock had just passed the tight ring of muscles, the flared tip stretching it wide as she fought to accustom herself to his large cock filling her there.

"More, baby?" he asked her, his hand smoothing down her back.

"More," she cried, her hips easing back on the burning lance. "More. Please, Cole. More."

He began to ease further inside her as the tip of Jesse's cock throbbed at the entrance to her cunt. A slow, steady stroke had Cole filling her ass completely, his hard groan as he sank into her to his balls echoed in the room.

Tess was crying out repeatedly now, her muscles clenching on him, her body accepting the pain as a torturous pleasure she couldn't deny any longer. Her hips moved against him, driving him deeper, lodging the pulsing head of Jesse's cock just inside her vaginal entrance as Cole pulled back, then pushed forward again.

"Yes," she screamed out as he began an easy thrusting motion inside her ass. "Oh God, Cole. Fuck me. Please fuck me!"

He pushed harder inside her. Once. Twice. Then stilled. Tess would have protested, but she lost her breath. Beneath her, Jesse began to push his hard cock into the tiny, tiny entrance of her vagina. Cole's cock filled her ass to bursting, leaving little room in her snug pussy. But Jesse didn't let that hinder him. Groaning, praising the ultra tight fit, he sank slowly into the heated depths until he was lodged in to the hilt.

Reality ceased to exist. She didn't even know when Jesse had reached up to release the leather manacles or when Cole had released those at her ankles. But she was on her hands and knees, sandwiched between them, begging for more. Pleading for the hard thrusts of their cocks inside her as they set up a slow, rhythmic thrusting motion that threatened to drown her in pleasure. She was insane with the burning ecstasy spearing her body. She moved against them, taking them, urging them on until their building thrusts were powerful strokes inside her. They were fucking her hard and fast now, each man groaning, praising her, crying out as she tightened on them.

"Cole," she screamed out his name as she felt her orgasm building. "Oh God, Cole, I can't stand it."

"You can, Tess," he groaned, levering over her body as his hips powered inside her. "You can, baby. Take it. Take it, Tess. Cum for me, baby. Cum for me now." He surged inside her as she tightened around him.

Beneath her, Jesse had clasped her waist hard, his hips slamming into hers, and despite their speed, both men kept in perfect synchronization with the hard thrusts of their cocks inside her body.

Tess couldn't stop her screams, couldn't stop the sensations that tightened her body, the boiling pressure, the hard, piercing pleasure/pain was too much for her untutored body to take for long. When she climaxed, she wailed out at the explosion, tightening on them further, her ass, her cunt milking the cocks possessing her until she heard their shattered male groans and felt the hard, spurting jets of their sperm filling each hole.

Her orgasm shuddered through her body, over and over. Her muscles clenched on their cocks as they exploded inside her, making them cry out around her, jerk against her as her cunt and her ass drew on their flesh, shuddered around it, burned them with her release until she fell against Jesse gasping, boneless.

"Son of a bitch, Cole," Jesse's voice was harsh, weary now. "She's drained me."

Cole pulled free of her and collapsed on the mattress, helping Jesse to lower Tess between them. Once there, he pulled her against his body, his hands running over her back, his lips caressing her temple as she fought to regain her breath.

"You're mine, Tess," he whispered, stopping her heart with the emotion she heard in his voice. "Taken by me. Held by me. I won't let you escape me again."

She would have answered him, but shock held her immobile when she heard the enraged scream of her mother from the doorway.

"You dirty whore! Just like your father. You're just like your father—!"

Chapter 11

"Oh my God!" Humiliation sped through Tess's system seconds later as Cole and Jesse jumped to hide her from sight.

They jerked their pants from the floor, shielding Tess as they dressed quickly. Cole's body was tight with fury as Tess fumbled with her gown, her fingers shaking so badly she could barely get it over her head.

Turning to her, still shielding her, Cole helped her untangle the material and ease it over her head.

"I'm sorry, baby," he whispered, his lips feathering over her hair as he straightened the gown.

Tess shook her head, feeling the heat that traveled over her face. With a final touch of his fingertips to her cheek, he turned to her mother.

"How the hell did you get in?" His voice was furious as he faced Ella Delacourte, dark and warning.

"I didn't come here to talk to you, perverted bastard that you are. Look how you corrupted my daughter. You're just like that trashy, home wrecking sister of yours." Ella was screeching now.

Tess felt her face flame in shame as she stood to her feet, her legs shaking from her exertions and her fear. Dear God, how had her mother got into the house?

"Mother, why are you here?" Tess's voice was thick with tears and confusion.

She wasn't ashamed that she had experienced the sexuality of the act. But being caught in it was mortifying. And by her mother!

"I came to see why you were here after I found out your father and his tramp were away for the week," she sneered. "You haven't even called me. I was worried."

The classic guilt trip from her mother any time Tess spent time with her father.

"Ella, control your tongue," Jesse's voice was hard and laced with warning.

Tess looked at him in surprise. She had no idea Jesse knew her mother.

Ella cast the other man a look that should have withered him with shame. Jesse stood before her, his shoulders squared, his dark face furious.

"Tess, go shower or something." Cole drew her into his arms, kissing her head softly, his hands soothing on her back. "Let me take care of this."

Tess shook her head.

"I haven't needed you to fight my battles before this, Cole. I don't need you to do it now," she said. "I haven't done anything wrong—"

"Wrong?" Ella's voice was piercing. "You think fucking your perverted lover and his friend isn't wrong, Tess? I raised you better than to whore for some depraved bastard."

Tess trembled at the fury in her mother's voice.

"Ella!" Jesse's voice was a lash of cold, hard fury now. "Get the hell out of here before I escort you out. And I don't think you want me to have to do that."

The heated edge of fury in Jesse's voice surprised Tess.

"Get her the hell out of here," Cole muttered to his friend.

"Would you guys just stop this?" Tess ran her fingers through her hair, hating the tremble in her hands as she faced her mother.

Years of being made to feel ashamed of her sexuality, of her needs as a woman washed over her. She remembered the lectures from the time she was a child, on the depravities of sex and the sins of the flesh.

"Mother, I told you I'd be back after the party," she sighed, leaning against Cole for support, thankful in a way that she didn't have to hide from her mother now.

"How could you do this, Tess?" Ella's expression was livid, her gray eyes glittering with fury. "How could you have become so depraved?"

"Depraved?" Tess shook her head, sighing. "I'm just different from you. I'm sorry."

A tear escaped her eyes. She hated having her mother angry with her, just as she had hated leaving her father so long ago.

As she finished speaking, a movement behind her mother caught Tess's attention. Her father, tall and strong, his face coldly furious, moved into the room.

"Well, I guess you're satisfied," Ella sneered when she saw him. "She's just like you and that whore you married."

Missy was with her father, and for once, Tess saw anger lining the beautiful blonde's face.

"You're in my home, Ella," Missy reminded her, her slender body tense and lined with anger. "I suggest you leave it and consider what you're losing in this display you seem intent on. Tess isn't a child. She's a woman. Her lifestyle is none of your concern."

Fury pulsed through the room, nearly choking Tess.

"I can't believe you did this. That a child of mine would lower herself to the same games her father plays." Tess flinched under the cold, unrelenting judgment her mother was meting out.

"Ella!" Missy's voice was a lash of hot fury. "I will have you escorted from my home if you cannot speak to your daughter decently. What she does is no business of yours. She's a grown woman."

"And I don't need anyone fighting my battles for me," Tess bit out, more than surprised at the confident edge of power in her stepmother's voice. Missy with a backbone? She wouldn't have believed it.

"Do you know what she was doing here, Jason?" Ella screamed out at her ex-husband. "This had gone even further than the games you practice —"

"For God's sake, Ella!" Jason cursed furiously. "Listen to you. Do you think our daughter wants to hear this? Our problems don't involve her." Her father's face was ruddy with his own embarrassment. "I don't care what she was doing. I trust Cole to protect her, that's all I needed to know."

"Well had you shown up a moment sooner —"

"Then I would have warned them of my arrival before entering the house," he growled in disgust as he cast Tess an apologetic look. "For pity's sake, stop humiliating Tess because of your own bitterness. This has gone too far."

Ella turned to Tess, her eyes hard, resentful. "Leave your belongings, Tess. You're going home with me. Now!"

When had she ever given her mother permission to order her around in such a manner? Tess watched her in growing confusion and pain. She had never known how angry, how bitter her mother had become. And for what reason? She had often stated how her life was more secure without a man interfering in it.

"I won't leave, Mother." She felt Cole's hands tighten at her shoulders, the way his body tensed expectantly behind her.

Shock filled her mother's expression.

"What did you say?" She seemed to gasp.

"I won't leave—"

"He's using you, Tess," Ella said furiously. "You'll be nothing but his whore. He proved that today."

Tess shook her head. "I love him, Mother. I have for years and I was too scared to admit to it. But I'm even more frightened of being alone and bitter, without at least having this time with him."

Silence held the room. She thought she heard Cole whisper a reverent "Thank God." But she wasn't certain.

"You will," Ella screamed furiously, her fists clenching at her side, her eyes glittering wildly. "You won't stay with these monsters."

"Perhaps it's where I belong." Tess wanted to cry out at the hurt that flashed in her mother's eyes. "I love Cole, Mother, and I'm not ashamed of that, or what I've done. I enjoyed it."

Ella opened her mouth to say more.

"Don't speak, Ella," Jason snapped. "Keep your mouth shut and leave her the hell alone."

"You don't control me, Jason," Ella bit out, her body trembling. "You didn't while we were married and you don't now."

"Probably what her problem is," Cole whispered at Tess's ear.

Her eyes widened for a moment before she put her elbow in his hard stomach. He only chuckled.

"I will if you don't keep that viperous tongue quiet," he growled. "And trust me, Ella, you better be careful. You may find out the monsters you hate so much are more a part of you than you know."

"I'm not part of this," Jesse finally sighed as he finished dressing. "I'm heading out of here, boys and girls. See you at the office, Cole."

He slapped Cole on the shoulder before leaving the room.

Ella's eyes followed him, narrowed, furious.

"Mother, perhaps you should leave as well." Tess took a hard, deep breath. "We'll discuss this later, when we're both calmer."

Ella turned back to her. The perfectly groomed cap of auburn hair framed a surprisingly young face. At forty-two, Ella Delacourte looked nearly a decade younger. But she was more bitter and vengeful than any woman twice her age, with a much harder life. "Come with me now, Tess, or I won't allow you back in my home." Ella's lips thinned as she stared at her daughter, ice coating her voice. "You'll no longer be a daughter of mine."

Tess trembled. She had never seen her mother so angry.

"I'm sorry, Mother." She shook her head. "I can't."

Ella drew herself erect. She cast her ex-husband a dark look then turned and stalked from the house. Tess flinched as the front door slammed closed behind her.

"She'll settle down, Tess," Jason said gently. "You know how your mother gets."

Tess ran her fingers through her hair as she took a hard, deep breath.

"She won't forgive me, Father," she said, her voice low, thick with tears. "Not ever. No more than she ever forgave you."

"Tess," Cole's voice was soft, gentle as his arms wrapped around her, holding her.

What a perfect feeling, she thought, to be held so tight, so warm against him. But how long would it last? How long could it last? She loved him, but how could he love her? Had her own desires, her unnatural needs lost her the love of the only man she had ever truly wanted?

Chapter 12

The question followed Tess through the rest of that night. Cole didn't come to her bed. For the first time in six nights, he wasn't beside her, tempting her, teasing her with his body, his lust. She lay in the middle of the big bed, staring silently up at the vaulted ceiling, the loneliness of the room smothering her. God help her, if she couldn't get through one night without him, how would she handle the rest of her life?

What had she done? Had her desire to experience with him everything his other women had been her downfall? Had her envy, her depravity, ruined the only chance she had to make him love her? She swallowed the tight knot of fear in her throat. Realistically, she had known that her chances of capturing his heart were slim. She just hadn't expected it to be over so soon.

Realizing she wouldn't be sleeping any time soon, Tess got up, pulling on the bronzed silk robe that lay at the bottom of the bed and belting it firmly. She slipped her feet into soft, matching slippers and left the room. She would prefer to sit in the kitchen, drowning her sorrows in the chocolate mint ice cream her father kept on hand, rather than wallowing in them.

As she stepped into the hallway, she followed the bright light spilling from the kitchen further up the hall. She halted in surprise at the doorway. Dressed in a thick robe, her blonde hair attractively mussed, her surprisingly pretty face free of makeup, sat Missy, digging into a bowl of the mint flavored chocolate, the box sitting temptingly in front of her.

"Great minds think alike?" Missy flashed her a smile as she looked up, waving the spoon in her hand at the cabinet. "Grab a bowl."

Tess walked to the cabinet and did just that, then sat down at the other side of the rounded table and began to spoon in a large portion.

"Nothing settles the nerves like Chocolate Mint," Missy sighed. "And I guess today rates as definitely that."

"I'm sorry," Tess apologized, genuinely regretful that she had caused her stepmother any pain. "I didn't expect Mother to show up."

Missy paused, her spoon suspended above her bowl as she flashed Tess a frown.

"Tess, I'm not upset for me," she said sincerely. "I'm upset for you and Cole. Your private choices should not be aired in such a manner. Cole was furious, of course, that she hurt you. But I was angry for your sake."

"Why?" Tess frowned. "We've never been close. We barely get along."

A knowing smile tipped Missy's pale lips.

"Tess, you fight with someone when you feel threatened, and when you care without a safety net, an assurance that you are cared for as well. I know that. I used to be the same way, until I met Jace."

Tess hunched her shoulders. Missy's assessment was much too close to the truth.

"That's how I knew you loved Cole." Missy dropped her next bombshell. "At first, it was just general sniping, but as he teased and flirted and pushed you, it became outright fighting on your side. I knew then your heart was involved."

Tess nearly choked on the spoonful of ice cream she was attempting to swallow. How could anyone, especially airhead Missy, who wasn't such an airhead after all, know her better than she knew herself?

"Have I lost him?" Tess couldn't keep the longing, the fear from her voice as she stared back at the other woman.

"Lost Cole?" Missy laughed in surprising amusement. "Tess, Cole has been fighting for your attention for over two years now. What the future will bring, I don't know. But I sincerely doubt you have anything to worry about for the present."

This did little ease to her worry.

"He hasn't returned." She shrugged, dropping her eyes to her bowl. "Maybe I disgusted him. Maybe I was supposed to refuse when Jesse came in?"

When Missy didn't answer, Tess risked a quick look.

The other woman watched her sympathetically, warmly.

"Cole is different from other men," she said as Tess watched her worriedly. "How different, is up to you to discover. But I've known him all his life, and I know Cole doesn't play games. If he invited Jesse, then he wanted it too. He wouldn't try to trap you, Tess, or hurt you. You have to trust him that far."

"I'm scared," Tess admitted, her eyes going back to the melting ice cream. "I don't know how to handle what I feel and what I want."

"Do any of us?" Missy's chuckle was self-mocking. "It takes meeting the man who can give us what we need, who knows, because it's what they need. I know, Tess, because that's what your father and I have. A relationship that fulfills what both of us need."

"Mother never loved him." Tess knew that, had known it for a long time.

"Your mother has to love herself first." Missy shrugged. "Now finish your ice cream. I'm sure Cole will be back before the party tomorrow, and he'll show you then how much he's missed you. I know he didn't want to leave and he hated going before talking to you first, but in this case, he assured me it was necessary."

What, Tess wondered, could have been so important that he couldn't even see her before leaving?

* * * * *

Tess waited, and she waited. All through the next day, while she was dressing for the party, and halfway through the boisterous, noisy affair she waited, and held onto the hope that he would be back that night. She gave up at nine. She set aside her glass of champagne, put away her hope and walked regally from the noisy ballroom and up the narrow steps that led to the Turret Room. She would pack and leave in the morning. She wasn't certain where she would go, but she was certain she couldn't risk staying here, or begging him to forgive her for something she didn't know if she would change.

The sexual dominance of the act had thrilled her. The utter thick, hot pleasure in Cole's voice had only spurred her on. She didn't know if it was something she would ever want again, but she knew experiencing it would be a memory she would always hold onto.

She kept her head down as she entered the room, going straight for the suitcase stored in the large walk-in closet just inside the room. She placed it on the luggage rack, opened it and re-entered the closet to collect the few things she had brought with her.

As she folded the articles of clothing, the tears began to fall. They were hot, blistering with pain, and shook her body as she tried to console herself that at least she had tried. For one time in her life, a very brief time, she was free.

She wiped at the tears, her breath hitching as she moved to the stone dresser and collect the clothing there, then she went to her bed and picked up her robe. The last article Cole had given her. It was then she saw the small, black velvet jewelers box. She stopped, clutching the silk robe to her chest

It was a ring. The diamond glittered with shards of blue and orange, intensifying the gold of the thick, simple band. Her hands shook, her body trembled. Her head raised, her eyes going to the shadows of the opened bathroom door.

"Shame on you, Tess," Cole chided her gently as he walked from the room where he waited. "To think I wouldn't come back. I'll have to punish you for that."

His chest was bare, his jeans rode low on his hips and fitted tightly over the bulge beneath the material.

Tess took a deep, hard breath.

"You didn't call," she whispered as she saw the mask of cool determination on his face, the sparkle of warmth in his eyes that was so at odds with his expression. "You didn't say goodbye."

"If I had seen you, I wouldn't have left. And I had to leave or miss the jeweler before he left. You should have known I had a reason."

Cole's voice was cool, disapproving. His eyes were patient, wicked and warm. God, she could feel her cunt heating to lava temperature.

"You knew I would worry," she snapped out, ignoring the hope, the happiness surging inside her.

"Worry, not have so little faith in me." There was an edge of hurt in his voice now, as though her tears, and the cause for them, pricked at his emotions. "After taking you, did you think I would let you go easily?"

A sob broke in her chest, another tear fell.

"I enjoyed it," she whispered brokenly. "You shouldn't love me."

"Tess," he whispered her name gently. "Don't you think I want it too? That I didn't enjoy your pleasure as well? It was the first time, baby, and it won't be the last time. I love hearing your cries, feeling your pleasure, knowing you're dominated, submitting to me, no matter what I want. Tess, I love you more for it, not less."

"How?" she whispered brokenly, shaking her head. "How could you?"

"Do you want Jesse alone, Tess?" he asked her carefully. "Would you let him touch you, hold you, if I didn't ask you to do so?"

"No!" she burst out, realizing the idea was abhorrent to her. What she had done with Cole could never have been done without him.

He came closer to her, standing within inches of her, staring down at her with heated arousal, and something more. Something she was terrified to admit to seeing. What if she was wrong? What if it wasn't love she saw in his eyes?

Rather than taking her in his arms, he indicated to her to sit on the bed. Tess did so slowly as he reached around her and retrieved the box on the bed. As her eyes rounded in shock, he went to one knee before her, holding the box in front of her as he stared up at her in adoration.

"You're mine." He wasn't asking her anything. "Taken by me, Tess. Mine to hold and mine to love now."

He took the ring from the box, picked up her hand and slid the diamond over her finger firmly.

"Is this a proposal?" she asked huskily, incredulously.

"Hell no. I'm not asking you anything," he grunted. "With that smart assed mouth of yours, you'd have me tying you down rather than loving you the way I want to."

"Loving me?" she whispered as he pushed her down on the bed, following her with his heated, hard body.

"Loving you, Tess," he promised. "With everything I have. With all I am, I love you."

His lips covered hers, his tongue pushing past her lips with a determination, a heat she couldn't deny. Her hands grasped his shoulders, her body arching to him as she groaned into the kiss. His lips ate at hers, his tongue plundering her mouth wickedly as his hands worked behind her back at the zipper of her dress, then stripped it quickly from her body.

He never broke the kiss, or lost the heat of his arousal as he stripped his pants from his hips, kicking them from his muscular legs. He didn't miss a beat as he ripped the silk of her panties from her body.

"Mine," he growled as his head finally raised, only to rake down her neck in a fiery caress, his tongue licking at her skin, his hands lifting her against him as they arrowed to her breast. There, his lips covered a hard, engorged nipple, sucking it into his mouth with a groan of arousal.

Tess arched to him, crying out brokenly at the fierce thrust of pleasure that clenched her womb and her vagina at the same time. Like a punch of heated ecstasy, her body bowed as he nibbled at the hard little point, his hand smoothing down her abdomen, his fingers parting the lips of her sex.

"Cole. Cole, please." She was on fire, needing his touch now more than she ever had.

"Say yes," he growled as his lips moved down her body, his tongue licking sensually, then his teeth nibbling with fierce, hot nips as he parted her thighs.

"Yes," she moaned, arching against him. "Yes, Cole. Anything. Just please don't stop."

He licked a slow, long stroke through the shallow valley of her cunt, his appreciation voiced in a low, long rumbling moan. His fingers parted her, his lips covered her clit with a heated suction that had her hips jerking sharply, arching to his mouth. Her knees bent, her thighs clenching around his head as he sucked and licked at the little pearl of nerves that throbbed almost painfully.

"So good," he growled, licking at her. "Delicious, Tess. But I need more, baby. Come for me. Come for me so I can love you the way I need to."

A finger, thick and long slid deep into her vagina, his mouth covered her clit, his tongue flickering in a wicked dance of pleasure as his finger filled her, retreated, then thrust inside her again. Tess bucked against him, her legs tightening around his head, her body heaving. Fire struck her loins, swelled her clit further, clenched her womb. The blood rushed through her body, carrying ecstasy, rapture, until she felt every particle of her being erupt against his mouth.

She was still crying, arching when he jerked her thighs apart and moved between them quickly.

"I love you, Tess," he whispered as he lowered himself against her, his cock, sliding against the lips of her sex, nudging inside them, then parting the tight muscles of her vagina.

"I love you," she whispered in return as the head of his cock parted her, slid in inch by inch, easing past the sensitive tissue, allowing her to feel every hard, hot, throbbing inch he was giving her. "Oh God, Cole, you'll kill me."

It was too much. He was too slow. The exquisite stretching, the slow stroke across nerve endings so sensitive, so desperate for relief, was taking her breath. Her head tossed on the bed, her hands slid across his sweat-dampened shoulders, then clenched in the silk of his hair.

"I'm loving you," he groaned. "Enjoy it, baby, it may not happen like this again for a while."

Torturous pleasure raged through her body. She could feel the clench of her vagina on the thick, hot shaft working gently inside her, the slow stretching, the hot brand of possession as he slid in to the hilt, then paused.

"Tess, baby," he whispered as he filled her, burying his face in her neck, his lips stroking her heatedly as he groaned.

She tightened the muscles of her vagina around his cock, whimpering at the heat, the searing sensations of near orgasm.

"I love you," she cried out again, holding him close, holding him tight. "I love you Cole, but I swear to God, if you don't fuck me right now, I'll kill you."

He didn't need a second urging. Bracing his knees on the mattress, he pulled back then slammed inside her. Tess screamed out at the rocketing, agonizing pleasure. Her back bowed, her legs curled around his hips, enclosing him in a vice as she fought to make him move harder, faster. She didn't have to urge him much.

With a harsh male cry of victory he began to thrust heatedly, heavily inside the slick heat of her body. Tess trembled at the onslaught of fiery sensations. Her vagina was stretched, filled, repeatedly stroked in hard, long thrusts that drove her higher, closer, strangling the breath in her throat as her release began to tear through her.

Like an orgasmic quake it rushed over her body, tightened her muscles and flung her from a precipice of agonizing need. Her cry echoed around her, distant, dazed as Cole gave one more gasping thrust then groaned out his release. She felt the hot, thick jets of his semen spurting inside her, filling her, completing her until she collapsed, boneless in his arms.

"Mine," he growled breathlessly as he fought to breath. "Now that I've taken you Tess, I won't let you go."

"Mm," she smiled tiredly. "Give me a minute and you can take again."

Cole chuckled tiredly, rolled from her and gathered her against his sweat-dampened chest.

"Sleep first," he grunted. "Then I'll dominate you some more."

"Or I could dominate you," she suggested with a smile. "Wake you up tied down. Torture you a little."

He gave her a worried look.

"Don't worry, baby," she imitated his slow, sexy drawl. "You'll love it."

The following excerpt from the short story "Wolfe's Hope", © Lora Leigh, 2002, is available in e-book format at http://www.ellorascave.com.

Prologue

July 1997, Genetics Council, Wolf Breed Labs
Mexico

Wolfe growled in fury, his teeth bared, his body taut, ready to spring as they pushed the young woman into his cell once again. She carried his scent now, proof that she was his mate. The mark he had given her the day before was still vividly evident on her upper shoulder.

"You'll do as I demand this time, Wolfe, or Hope will take the beating instead of you," Delia Bainesmith told him coldly.

"She's your daughter," he howled out in fury. "How can you do this to her?"

"She is a lab rat, no more, no less than are you," she informed him smugly. "Now breed her. She's ovulating, and we've made certain she's ready. Fuck her, my little wolf, or she'll be the one who pays."

The Bitch walked away, her laughter echoed behind her as Hope whimpered in sexual distress. They had given her an aphrodisiac, ensuring she would accept him.

"Please, Wolfe." Her slender body shook with tremors of arousal. "It hurts."

"I can't, Hope." He couldn't look at her. "I won't."

She was just a child, barely seventeen. He wouldn't scar her, either physically or emotionally with what he knew was coming.

"She'll beat me," she whispered.

"She won't get the chance." He knew that.

"She said you mated with me. How did you mate with me, without taking me?"

He could almost hear the tears whispering over her pale cheeks.

"I marked you, Hope." He couldn't stop his eyes from going to the proof of his ownership. "No other will touch you. No other will have you. That mark and the scent it places on you is mine alone. Don't make the mistake of ever allowing another man in your bed. Because I'll kill him."

Cold, hard rage shuddered through him at the thought. He had killed one soldier already over her. The one who had dared to fondle her breasts as they tore her clothes from her the day before.

"I'm sorry she did this. It's my fault, for loving you." As always, she would try to take the blame on her slender shoulders.

"No, Hope, it is my fault," he told her bleakly. "Mine for ever desiring to try to hope for more."

*****

Explosions ripped through the compound. Gunfire exploded around the small house Hope was locked into; the smell of burning buildings, the sounds of horrified screams echoed in her head.

"Wolfe!" She screamed his name out. Huddled in the bedroom on the opposite end of the house, terrified it would go up in flames at any minute, she prayed he would find her.

The ground rocked, plaster showered from the roof as she pressed herself closer to the huge dresser that she prayed would deflect the ceiling should it fall. She screamed out Wolfe's name again. He would come for her soon.

The sound of the front door slamming had her on her feet, racing for the doorway. Her abrupt halt just inside the living room had her rocking on her heels. Her mother stood there, furious, shaking, her normally austere composure crumpled.

"Wolfe," Hope couldn't stop her cry, her unasked question.

"The son of a bitch is dead. They all are," she sneered. "They hit the Labs first, and it's an inferno. Forget it, Hope, save yourself now. Don't worry about that mongrel excuse for a man."

Hope slid to the floor, the wall supporting her body, her mind unable to accept, unable to process the meaning of her mother's words.

"He'll come for me," she whispered.

Cruelty echoed in Delia Bainesmith's demented laughter.

"Wishful thinking, daughter. That bastard will never cum again. Too bad. You might have enjoyed it."

Chapter 1

Six Years Later, July 2002
Albuquerque, New Mexico

Hope Bainesmith knew when she received the phone call from her mother that it wasn't going to be a good day. The woman hadn't bothered to call her for years, had taken no interest in her life other than the monthly medical tests Hope was required to take. So the phone call that morning had caused her no small amount of concern.

"Have you seen Wolfe?" Hope's knees had weakened at the question. She collapsed into the kitchen chair, stilling the pain that raged in her chest.

Wolfe. Her hand touched the mark at her upper shoulder. Her body throbbed in remembrance. It was that mark that made the monthly tests necessary. An odd quirk of nature, given to a man that was created by science. The small bite had allowed a minute amount of an unknown hormone into her blood. It marked her pheromones and acted as a very mild aphrodisiac. She had been in arousal hell ever since. Hence the reason for monthly medicals.

"Wolfe's dead, mother. Remember?" She reminded the creature who spawned her. "How could I see him?"

There was silence over the line. Hope knew her voice reflected the grief she still lived with on a daily basis. It had been nearly six years but she could still remember with brutal clarity the attack on the Labs, the engulfing blaze and the horrendous screams from those trapped inside.

"We never recovered a body," Dr. Bainesmith reminded her, her cultured voice cool and autocratic.

Hope could just see her petite, pretty mother, her black eyes as cold as ice, her Asian features a cool mask of studied indifference. Nothing mattered but the project at hand, and nothing else would matter. But Wolfe wasn't a project anymore, she wanted to scream, and neither was she.

"There were a lot of bodies you didn't recover," Hope pointed out painfully. "Wolfe's dead, let him rest in peace now."

She hung up the phone carefully, fighting the tears that filled her eyes. The instinctive longing welled inside her at the oddest times. Wolfe was dead. No amount of grieving could bring him back. There was no justice to be found — no matter what she did — in his death.

Her mother refused to accept it. Wolfe was *her* creation; she considered him and his Pack *her* property. He had defeated her with his death, and Hope knew the other woman could not accept that she would no longer command the army she had envisioned. A pack of savage, intelligent soldiers with the instincts and intelligence of an animal.

The world was still in shock, even now, years after the broadcast of the first Breeds, felines in that case, announcing their lives. Those men and women, created by science, had been genetically altered with the DNA of savage cats. They had been created to kill. "Disposable soldiers," one announcer had reported. The Breeds they were called, for want of a better name. It was during the broadcast of that announcement that the labs in Mexico had been raided by Mexican and American agents. It had been a brutal, bloody battle, one that would have done any drug lord proud. But it wasn't drugs they sought; it was the human experimentations and the scientists and soldiers who made their lives hell that the agents wanted.

Hope shuddered at the memories of screams, the erupting flames and gunfire echoing around the house she hid in. She had screamed Wolfe's name over and over during those hours. Certain he would have escaped. But had he escaped, he would surely have come for her. He had claimed her, swore she belonged to him.

He wouldn't have left her there to die.

About the authors:

Jaid Black and Lora Leigh might have different writing styles, but both best-selling novelists are celebrated by erotic romance fans for the same reasons: they are prolific, they write stories hot enough to burn, and readers can't get enough of their controversial, imaginative tales.

Jaid and Lora welcome mail from readers. You can write to them c/o Ellora's Cave Publishing at P.O. Box 787, Hudson, OH 44236-0787. For a full listing of their available titles please write to Ellora's Cave Publishing via mail or visit us on the web at http://ellorascave.com.

Why an electronic book?

We live in the Information Age—an exciting time in the history of human civilization in which technology rules supreme and continues to progress in leaps and bounds every minute of every hour of every day. For a multitude of reasons, more and more avid literary fans are opting to purchase e-books instead of paperbacks. The question to those not yet initiated to the world of electronic reading is simply: why?

1. *Price.* An electronic title at Ellora's Cave Publishing runs anywhere from 40-75% less than the cover price of the <u>exact same title</u> in paperback format. Why? Cold mathematics. It is less expensive to publish an e-book than it is to publish a paperback, so the savings are passed along to the consumer.

2. *Space.* Running out of room to house your paperback books? That is one worry you will never have with electronic novels. For a low one-time cost, you can purchase a handheld computer designed specifically for e-reading purposes. Many e-readers are larger than the average handheld, giving you plenty of screen room. Better yet, hundreds of titles can be stored within your new library—a single microchip. (Please note that EC does not endorse any specific brands. You can check our website for customer recommendations we make available to new consumers.)

3. *Mobility.* Because your new library now consists of only a microchip, your entire cache of books can be taken with you wherever you go.

4. *Personal preferences are accounted for.* Are the words you are currently reading too small? Too large? Too...**ANNOYING**? Paperback books cannot be modified according to personal preferences, but e-books can.

5. *Innovation.* The way you read a book is not the only advancement the Information Age has gifted the literary community with. There is also the factor of what you can read. Ellora's Cave Publishing will be introducing a new line of interactive titles that are available in e-book format only.

6. *Instant gratification.* Is it the middle of the night and all the bookstores are closed? Are you tired of waiting days—sometimes weeks—for online and offline bookstores to ship the novels you bought? Ellora's Cave Publishing sells instantaneous downloads 24 hours a day, 7 days a week, 365 days a year. Our e-book delivery system is 100% automated, meaning your order is filled as soon as you pay for it.

Those are a few of the top reasons why electronic novels are displacing paperbacks for many an avid reader. Welcome to the Information Age!

As always, Ellora's Cave Publishing welcomes your questions and comments. We invite you to email us at service@ellorascave.com or write to us directly at: P.O. Box 787, Hudson, Ohio 44236-0787.

Printed in the United States
59442LVS00001B/349-396